Constance Smith

The Repentance of Paul Wentworth

A novel. Vol. 3

Constance Smith

The Repentance of Paul Wentworth
A novel. Vol. 3

ISBN/EAN: 9783337315733

Printed in Europe, USA, Canada, Australia, Japan

Cover: Foto ©Andreas Hilbeck / pixelio.de

More available books at **www.hansebooks.com**

THE REPENTANCE

OF

PAUL WENTWORTH.

A Novel.

IN THREE VOLUMES.

VOL. III.

LONDON:

RICHARD BENTLEY AND SON,

Publishers in Ordinary to Her Majesty the Queen.

1889.

" Men are led by strange ways. One should have tolerance for a man, hope of him; leave him to try yet what he will do."—CARLYLE.

CONTENTS OF VOL. III.

THE REPENTANCE

OF

PAUL WENTWORTH.

CHAPTER I.

CONTENT?

"Color che son contenti
Nel fuoco, perchè speran di venire
Quando che sia, alle beate genti."
DANTE, *Inferno*, I.

A DARK dull afternoon late in November. Overhead, a leaden, low-hanging sky, which at the
extreme edge of the horizon seemed to melt into
and become confounded with the great rolling
expanse of a wide Leicestershire plain; under-
foot, long stretches of muddy road, and flat
soaked meadows out of which the incessant rain
of weeks past appeared to have washed their very
greenness, where it had not actually converted

them into cold, unlovely lakes.   Every brook for miles round was swollen temporarily to the dimensions of a river.   On all sides were to be seen broad, yellow, turbid streams, moving sluggishly among sedges, reeds, and scattered willows to their confluence with others like unto themselves; when, for all their apparent sluggishness, they overflowed their banks, obliterating hedges and gates and familiar landmarks, and dealing around them a vast amount of silent mischief. The atmosphere was filled with a subtle mist, not sufficiently dense to be called a fog, nor wet enough to be dignified by the name of rain, but which nevertheless hung heavily and visibly on every tree and bush and wayside hedgerow, blotting out the last touches of autumn colour which still lingered there with the remaining leaves and gave its only possible suggestion of beauty to this most unattractive landscape.

An unattractive landscape it was, brooded over by a most unattractive day; consequently, there were few people abroad whose business did not force them away from their warm firesides. Even the party of hunting men who had ridden out from Clayburn Hall that morning on their way to a distant meet, ardent devotees of the chase as they one and all were, had started half reluctantly; and at four o'clock the roads were almost deserted, save for an occasional passing farm-cart, and a stray child or two returning to some distant hamlet from school. Muriel Arlingham, sallying forth for a late afternoon's walk on such a miserable day, was tolerably secure of the solitude she craved.

Not that she desired solitude for purposes of reflection. Far from it. She had had ample time already for that unpleasant exercise, after her husband had flung angrily away to join his hunting friends at the close of another fruitless, disheartening interview; she had had the whole of a long morning in her own room, while her hostess supposed her to be busy writing letters, and so good-naturedly forbore to disturb her. She knew she should have time enough and to spare in those still longer night-watches when oblivion would refuse to come at her bidding, and all the mocking ghosts of the dead past, all the miserable presentiments of the menacing future, which she managed after a fashion to exorcise and keep at bay during daylight hours, would crowd upon her unsleeping vision. No, she had not come out to think, nor even to try and distract her thoughts, but for a more prosaic and unromantic reason. She was not a woman given to tears as a rule, but a new grief added to her sum of trouble, and realized for the first time that day, had sufficed to let loose an unwonted tempest. Naturally, she did not wish her friends to see that she had been crying; so she came out to try that peculiarly English specific for an aching heart and wounded spirit —a long country walk.

Her way lay over a couple of fields—less low-lying or better drained than the rest, for they were comparatively dry—where a well-kept footpath led from the Clayburn demesne to the highroad, and finally to the village, a forlorn little cluster of houses grouped round an old square-towered Norman church, about a mile off. Just before crossing the road, the field-path described an abrupt curve at the corner of a little closely set plantation of oak and fir, and at the end of the curve was a small iron swing gate. Muriel, rounding the corner with the peculiarly swift light walk which had been hers from childhood, the step of a woman accustomed to the wide spaces, the open air, and free movement of country life, almost ran against a man who was leaning over this gate in a contemplative fashion, with a bundle of letters in his hand.

She recovered herself with a hasty " I beg your

pardon!" Before the words were out of her mouth, the gentleman against whom she had been within an ace of jostling so unceremoniously was lifting his hat with a dawning smile of recognition; as she ceased to utter them, she found that she was standing face to face with Philip Irvine.

The sight of him was a kind of shock to her. She had not seen him for more than three years; not since the morning when by his counsels he had unwittingly fixed her destiny in life; and his sudden apparition reminded her of more than she cared to remember. But she betrayed nothing of all this in her manner.

"I am immensely surprised to see you," she said, " though I am very glad to do so. I don't know why I say I am surprised, either; it is quite as natural that you should be here as I. Only it is so long since we met, and it seems strange to meet you at last in a Leicestershire lane, since it is hardly likely that you have come down to hunt ! "

"No," Irvine answered with one of his grave smiles. " I had business in the north, and on my way home I am spending a couple of days with an uncle of mine, who is rector of a parish about two miles from this. I walked over to the post-town for the second post, as my uncle

contents himself with one batch a day, and I
had just halted to glance through some of my
letters when you came up. I am glad to see you
looking so well, Mrs. Arlingham."

He did not express any pleasure at meeting
her. The renewal of their acquaintance gave
him indeed no special pleasure, and did give him
a certain amount of not altogether unaccountable pain. His steady determination for two
years past not to renew it, was due to other
causes than a mere disapproval of Muriel's eager
participation in what he considered the sinful
frivolities of fashionable life.

"Yes, thank you, I am very well," Muriel
answered, with a scarcely repressed sigh. There
were times when she almost hated her own
health and strength, and the consciousness of
physical youth which was as an earnest of long
years of life to come. And already, at twenty-
three, she was so tired of life, so tired!

"Mr. Arlingham is well too, I hope?" pur-
sued Irvine courteously. "No doubt he is here
for hunting purposes?"

"My husband is quite well, thanks. Yes, he
is enjoying his stay in the Shires very much.
We have been paying rather a long visit to the
Merediths, the good people up yonder, but our

time is up next Monday. Then we are going —I don't know exactly where. Mr. Arlingham has not quite made up his mind."

There was a sort of dull patience, a repressed pain in Muriel's voice which struck Irvine's ear and roused his sympathies. He could hardly have told why, but instinctively he felt sorry for her. Perhaps he might have proceeded to make a shrewd guess at the nature of her trouble, had he not been busy with a more personally interesting question—namely, how to put to her a question he both longed and feared to ask. Before he could frame his query in what he judged to be fitting words, Muriel spoke again.

" By-the-by, I am glad to have an opportunity of reproaching you," she said. " Why have you never been to see us in town, Mr. Irvine ? We expected you fully for a long time, but at length we had perforce to resign expectation. Let me hear your excuses."

" You know, I think, that I don't visit much. I am rather a busy man, Mrs. Arlingham ; and among your friends I should be more or less out of place, I fear."

Muriel flushed slightly. " We are mere butter-flies in your estimation, I know," she answered, half bitterly, half sadly. "But all my friends are not butterflies, I assure you; and there are times when I am actually serious myself! Your sister would vouch for so much as that, I think."

Irvine's stern lips relaxed a little. "Margaret is very much attached to you," he said. "I often hear of you from her. I believe you spent part of last summer together, did you not?"

"Part of the autumn, rather. I was not quite the thing when we came back from a yachting expedition towards the end of August, and they said I wanted quiet. Too much gaiety, I suppose!"—with a curious semi-defiant glance at Irvine's severe face. "Margaret was more sympathizing than you would have been in such a case. She knew that in most people's houses, or even at home, I should have other guests or visitors to bore me to death: so she just came and carried me off with her to Devonshire, where I had a month of real rest. What peace and delight it was, every day of it!"

"I am glad you enjoyed it," Irvine said kindly, softened in spite of himself. "It was a great pleasure to Margaret, I know; and her life, though a fully occupied one, is lonely in some respects. She does not make friends very easily, but she looks upon you as a real friend."

"Her friendship is of infinite value to me," Muriel replied. "I cannot tell you how much I have learnt from her, or how she helps me—unconsciously very often—every time I see her." Then, with a recurrence of the impulse which had come upon her once before, and which came to so many people in this man's presence—an impulse to go beneath the surface of things, and exchange conventionalities for realities—she added, "The farther one advances in life, the more one needs help of this kind. Such help you gave me once yourself."

"I am glad to think so," Irvine responded gravely.

"Not that I used your counsel rightly at first," Muriel went on eagerly, as if it were a relief to speak, even by implication, of something higher and deeper than the subjects which formed the usual topics of conversation with her now. "At first I misapplied it; I made terrible mistakes through my own impatience and wilfulness, and then for a time I was inclined to be angry with you"—smiling faintly. "But at last I am beginning to learn, slowly perhaps, yet I do think surely, the real meaning of what you taught me so long ago."

There was a little quiver in Muriel's voice as

she concluded, but she had been looking straight at Irvine all the while she addressed him. As in her girlhood, so now, she felt an utter absence of shyness and self-consciousness in speaking thus freely to this young man whom she knew so slightly, but to whom all the spiritual part of her went out in instantaneous sympathy. Neither did any curious element in this relation between them seem to strike him either.

"I am heartily thankful to hear you say this," he answered with a beautiful light in his eyes. "If it is the lesson of endurance and self-sacrifice that you are learning, you will do well and safely, Mrs. Arlingham. Forgive me for having supposed that it was otherwise with you."

"You had every excuse for thinking so," Muriel rejoined quickly. "I don't seem to people in general much like a person who is learning any lesson at all, except how best to amuse myself, do I? Mr. Irvine!"—with sudden, passionate earnestness—"give me your experience. I know you always choose the harder path for yourself, as you advised me to do. Does your choice satisfy you? Are you content with it?"

Philip Irvine drew a long breath before he answered slowly, "I think I may truthfully say

I am. There are times with us all when the spirit of unbelief and rebellion is strong for a while. But at the worst moments I do not *regret;* I would not undo anything of the past. God has given me to feel that I could have done no otherwise."

Muriel's question had been a general one; Irvine's answer related rather to the supreme sacrifice of his life, the sacrifice consummated one summer morning, more than three years ago, in the drawing-room of the old Holmshire Manor House. But his secret was still unknown to every human being save himself—and one other, who had kept it so safely shrouded in a mantle of sacred silence that not even her nearest and dearest had been able to guess at its existence. So now Muriel only said, "Thank you for answering a question which I fear I was presumptuous in asking. Some day perhaps, when I am more fit for it and more worthy of it, that content will come to me too." She stopped, and held out her hand to end the interview. After the words that had just passed between her and Irvine, it would have seemed utterly incongruous to return to the banalities of everyday small-talk.

But the young man ignored the proffered

hand. "Must you go? Are you in a hurry?" he asked, with a nervous eagerness quite foreign to his usual cold, grave manner. "You have not yet told me about your people in Holmshire. How are they all?"

Muriel's face grew troubled, though she only said, "My father is extremely well, thanks. He has been made very happy lately by a visit from George, who is home from India on a three months' furlough. Of course you know George is married now? His wife is a charming girl; we are all delighted with her. They sail again the week after next, I am sorry to say."

"And your sister? She is well too?"

The suggestion of trouble in Muriel's face deepened. "No, indeed, she is far from well; we are very uneasy about her. She is going out to India with George and his wife on the seventh; all the doctors say it is her best chance, and we try to hope everything from it. But we are very, very anxious."

Philip Irvine turned deadly white, but he uttered no word of regret or sympathy. "I had heard nothing of this," he said. "Has she been ill long?"

"We thought not, at first; but now, looking back, it seems to me as if this had been coming

upon her gradually for a long, long while. Oh,
Mr. Irvine, how is it that one is always so
blind—that one never sees these things in
time ? "

" How came it to pass that you did not see ? "
he asked sharply, almost fiercely. His own pain
was so great that he could not think of Muriel's ;
and the idea of Lucy drooping and dying by
slow degrees unobserved maddened him against
those whose duty it was to have watched over
her.

"I was not there," Muriel answered gently.
" My father—well, men are so slow to notice
little ailments " ("I should have seen quickly
enough ! " Irvine thought bitterly to himself),
" and my cousin, whom you remember, was
away nursing in one of the hospitals for two
years after I left home. And Lucy always said
it was nothing, nothing ! It was only a cold, or
she was overtired, or some such little unselfish
excuse to keep us from being anxious. She is
very different from what she used to be," the
sister added with regretful tenderness; " much
more grave, and serious, and thoughtful; though
even now, at times, she is full of life and spirit.
You know she was always so bright in those old
days."

"And how long is it since this illness began?" Irvine demanded in a harsh, inquisitorial tone, fixing his blue eyes, which in the last few moments had grown colourless and hard, full on Muriel's sad face. "What do you call long, Mrs. Arlingham? Months, or weeks?"

"Rather years than months," Muriel replied, half frightened by his imperious manner and inexplicable agitation. "It must be quite three years since she first began to ail something, though we hardly knew what. I don't think she was ever quite well after the summer of three years ago. You remember—that very hot summer when you came down to stay with us?"

God help him! he remembered only too well. For a minute he felt as if he had been told that he had killed Lucy; and he stood gazing at Muriel, white and silent.

At length he managed to say hoarsely, "You are not without hope?"

"Oh no, no!" Muriel answered eagerly, with a horrified shrinking from the bare idea of hopelessness. "It is not consumption, you know; only a kind of failure of strength, and a bad cough, so that the doctors think the consequences might be serious if she stayed in England. We quite hope two or three years in India will make her well and strong again."

"You are not going with her?"

"I? Oh no! I could not, you see; it would be quite impossible." She could have smiled to herself in bitterness at the simplicity of the question, as she recalled the cutting words and stubborn objections she had encountered that very morning when craving permission to spend a few days with Lucy before she left England, merely because the projected visit happened to interfere with some unimportant arrangement of her husband's. "My sister-in-law will be very good to her," she added, feeling vaguely sorry for her companion. "She is devoted to Lucy, and Lucy looks upon her as if she were her own sister already."

"I am glad of that," Irvine answered briefly and with effort. "And now I must say good-bye; you will believe that I feel very deeply, more deeply than I can say, for you all in this trouble and anxiety. You will be seeing your sister soon, doubtless?"

"Next week, probably."

"When you see her, will you tell her something from me? I should like her to know——" He came to a dead stop suddenly.

"Yes?" said Muriel interrogatively. "She will be glad to hear of you again, I am sure. What is the message?"

A sort of spasm shook Irvine's impassive face for a moment. "No," he said more decidedly. "On second thoughts, I will not send a message; better so, perhaps. Good-bye, Mrs. Arlingham. May God help and bless her! I dare not say more."

Muriel left her hand in his for a minute. "Thank you for being so sorry for her," she said in her old childlike way. "And—you won't forget her in your prayers, will you? She will like to know she has those now."

Irvine was actually turning away; but at Muriel's last words he looked back. "Those she has had always," he answered. "You may tell her that, if you will."

Then he went rapidly away down the dark wet road, where the thick enveloping mist-pall soon shrouded him completely from sight; and Muriel turned and wandered slowly back to the house she had lately quitted. She had forgotten all about her projected walk.

CHAPTER II.

"SWEET IS TRUE LOVE."

"Not all unhappy, having loved God's best
And highest."

TENNYSON.

A WEEK had gone by, and Muriel was sitting with Lucy in the drawing-room at Alderton. There were winter berries instead of summer blossoms in the old china flower-bowls, and a great wood fire sparkled and crackled on the hearth; otherwise the picturesque, comfortable, home-like room was quite unchanged. It was growing late in the evening. Mr. Ferrars and his son were safely ensconced in the smoking-room, and George's pretty, tender-hearted little wife had made some kindly excuse about "going to sit beside baby," in order to leave the two sisters to themselves for an hour. And well as they loved her, they were glad of the *tête-à-tête*, during which they could either talk or sit on in silence, with no light but that of the leaping flames, happy in that perfect sympathy which has no need of words. Muriel leaned back in the old familiar tapestry-covered armchair, and tried to fancy herself a girl again; while Lucy, half sitting, half lying on the hearthrug, with her thin flushed cheek resting against Muriel's knee, gazed quietly into the glowing embers, and smiled now and again to herself a smile which bespoke at once a little sadness and a great content.

At length the clock struck eleven, and Muriel roused herself from her reverie. "You ought to be going upstairs, dear," she said. "I am a miserable nurse to have kept you up so late."

"Oh, I very rarely go to bed early," Lucy rejoined cheerfully. "Never if I can possibly help it; the early part of the night is always my worst time. And I have heaps of things to ask you still, Queenie"—using an old fond childish appellation which had not fallen upon Muriel's ears for years past. "Tell me a little more of your doings this summer."

"There is not much to tell. One country-house visit is so like another, when one comes to try and describe it; especially to you who

don't know the people. (After all, they are
generally very much alike too.) And all the
time we were yachting round Norway I was ill
and out of sorts, and incapable of enjoying things.
I think I must have been stupid with illness; I
hardly remember anything about it now."

"Poor Queenie!" Lucy said softly, slipping
one hand—a hand which felt, oh, so terribly
light and small—into her sister's. "But you
are quite well again ?"

"Quite well and quite strong. I began to get
better from the day that I went to Margaret
Irvine's."

"Margaret is one of the sweetest women I
know!" Lucy exclaimed with grateful enthusiasm. "I delighted in her as soon as I saw her.
And she is the right sort of friend for you: she
appreciates you as few people can."

"She thinks a good deal more of me than I
deserve, I am afraid; but anyhow, her goodness
to me this autumn was unutterable. That month
in Devonshire was a veritable little heaven of
peace, Lucy."

Muriel was not aware how much that last
impulsive sentence of hers betrayed of the un-
peaceful character of her everyday life. Lucy,
who grasped its meaning well enough, had never-

theless far too much wisdom and fine tact to let
it appear that she did so.

"Were you alone with Miss Irvine all through
September?" she asked.

"Except for the two children, who were no
trouble to either of us. She would not ask any
one else."

"What children do you mean? Those nieces
I saw at her house one day?"

"Yes: Stella and Mabel Wentworth. Their
father went to Russia in August for a vacation
tour, and left them with Margaret, as he does
very frequently."

"Are they nice girls?"

"Scarcely more than children as yet, though
Stella is all but sixteen. She is very impressionable and warm-hearted and lovable; I grew very
fond of her. Mabel is colder and less childlike,
somehow, though she is younger than her sister."
Muriel looked thoughtfully into the fire. "Stella
grew very fond of me too," she added after a
minute, half to herself. "Hers is a very loving
nature, I think."

As she spoke, there rose up vividly before her
the remembrance of long golden September afternoons when Stella, with her pretty coaxing ways,
would caressingly insist on her dearest Mrs.

Arlingham's coming to sit with her uuder the
great beech tree which overshadowed MissIrvine's
little lawn, in order that, in the absence of aunt
and sister alike, she might the better be able to
engross wholly the attention of her new and
enthusiastically worshipped friend; and of how
the girl would lie there for hours at her feet,
pouring out tales of the past, rhapsodies of the
present, impossible visions of the future, with
the natural eloquence she had learnt from Wentworth, brightened now and then by a touch of
his sparkling wit. She remembered how closely
his name was interwoven with every history and
reminiscence and plan of his young daughter's;
and how, as Stella talked on, she had found
herself learning more and more of that "other
side of the shield" hidden from public gaze: of
Wentworth's tender patience and sweet temper
and unfailing forbearance with the children who
adored him so selfishly (since when was not a
spoilt child's unreasoning, unreasonable love
more or less selfish?); of that deep reverence
for high and sacred things which was so strange
and yet so powerful an element in his wayward,
complex nature; of the quick sympathies which
had again and again prompted him to acts of
almost Quixotic generosity utterly unknown to

the world at large; and of the innate chivalry which enabled him to perform those acts with such thoughtful delicacy and forgetfulness of self, that the very recipients of his kindness only realized with difficulty the fact that anything had been done for them at all. And with the remembrance of these things came the old secret thrill of irrepressible pride and delight which the hearing of them had wrought in her, followed by the swift keen stab of self-reproach which was its natural sequel. She knew that she had listened readily, far too readily, to Stella's innocent chatter on those sunny September afternoons, and that when, in momentary compunction, she had checked or turned the conversation, it had been with half-hearted resolution only, knowing that the young devotee would soon wander round again to the old fascinating subject. For "my father" was the centre of Stella's world, the prince and hero of her fond, faithful, implicit devotion; he was her knight *sans peur et sans reproche*, the cleverest, handsomest, noblest of the sons of men. She worshipped him with a single-hearted loyalty and a blind fanaticism which saw in him neither fault nor flaw; in her eyes he was one peerless, having neither equal nor second among any that walk this nether earth.

Muriel shook herself free of that pleasant, painful, self-accusing recollection with a little sigh.

" By the way," she said, " when I was at Clayburn, I saw some one we all used to know in the old days—Mr. Irvine. We met quite accidentally. I was out for a walk one horrible foggy day, when I encountered him going over to the post-town from a neighbouring village. I was really glad to see him again."

Lucy said nothing; her one care for the moment was to keep perfectly still. If only she could get her hand out of Muriel's! If only her heart would not beat so that she dared not attempt a single question!

" His never calling on me in London was rather uncivil, of course," Muriel went on serenely; " or rather, it would have been uncivil in any one else. Somehow one never thinks of judging Philip Irvine by ordinary standards. He is not quite like other people, you know."

No, very unlike; Lucy knew that well enough. If only she could get breath enough to say so, or to say anything!

" I spoke to him about his omission," Muriel continued, " but not as if I was offended—which, indeed, I am not in the least."

"What did he say?" Lucy forced out the four words in a curious strained voice.

"Oh, he answered me much as I expected him to do; he made no excuses, but gave some reason, I forget exactly what, such as only he would have thought of giving. I wish I could remember how he put it, but I have forgotten."

She had forgotten! After three years and a half of silence, three years and a half of that deadly hunger for tidings of a word or a look of Philip Irvine's which nothing had ever come to satisfy, Muriel had met him and talked with him —and forgotten what he said! It was hard, bitterly hard. But Lucy gave no expression to her feeling. She only withdrew her hand from her sister's, picked up a newspaper that lay on the rug beside her, and folded it into the form of a fire-screen as well as her shaking fingers would allow. Then she leant back again, and asked, in as steady a voice as she could command, "Was Mr. Irvine looking well?"

"Yes—no. He has grown thinner than he used to be; still, he seemed very well. You know he was always pale, and then that long throat of his—do you remember?"

Yes, Lucy remembered.

"Well, owing to his thinness, he has rather an

appearance now of being all throat and eyes ; but he must be strong. His is a trying life, such as only a strong man could lead."

" It needs strength every way," Lucy returned brusquely. Then she paused and waited for more.

Muriel looked at her counsellor, the fire, for a moment before speaking again. Then she put her hand softly on the dark head at her knee. " Lucy," she said timidly, " had you ever any idea that Mr. Irvine cared for you ? "

The girl started violently, and then made a desperate effort to recover herself. " Why do you ask ? " she inquired. " Has he—has he spoken of me to you ? "

" He asked after you, and of course I had to tell him of your illness, and that you were going to India. Then I saw how it was with him. It was not mere regret, nor kindly feeling, nor sympathy for me that I could see in his face; it was such grief as a man only feels when he loves—and loves very dearly," Muriel added pityingly. " Poor fellow ! I was sorry for him, Lucy, truly."

Lucy lay still, hardly knowing whether joy or pain was uppermost with her.

" Did you never guess anything of this ? " Muriel asked again.

Then for the first time the girl lifted her head and looked at her sister, with a glad, proud light in her eyes. " Yes, I knew," she answered simply. "He did not mean me to know, but I found it out ; and then he told me."

"But you do not care for him?" Muriel pleaded appealingly. "You have not been dreaming of him all this while, Lucy? I could not surely have been so blind as that !"

"I meant you to remain blind," replied Lucy quietly. "I hardly know why I have told you now."

"Then it is so? And it is that which has altered you so, my darling !"

"Do you think it has altered me for the worse?" said Lucy, with a faint reflection of one of Irvine's own smiles. "Muriel, listen. If there is one thing in my life for which I thank God night and morning—yes, and many times in every day too!—it is for having known *him*, and for the knowledge that he loves me." ·

"A love which has brought you nothing but sorrow," Muriel said bitterly. She rebelled vehemently against the thought of suffering as Lucy's portion, though she was learning to accept it quietly as her own. "What right had he to let you know of its existence, if it was out of his power to make you happy by it?"

"Did I not tell you that he never intended me to know? I found it out one day, without his speaking a word. Was he to blame for that? Only, when he knew that I had found it out, he was too brave and true to go away and leave me to uncertainty and misconception, and so he told me all. And I was never so proud of him as at that minute."

"He is a good man, I know," said Muriel, still bitterly. "Only I wish he would not have spoilt your life with his goodness."

"Say rather that he taught me by his example what life really was, and what might be made of it. I would not have had him act otherwise; I am quite sure of that now. But even when I was most unhappy, when he first went and left me, I think I could hardly have been glad if he had elected to come back and give up his work for my sake. He would never have been quite the same in my eyes again. I wanted him to be perfect, you see; I should not have felt satisfied for him to be less than perfect."

"I cannot quite see the need of such a sacrifice."

"Cannot you? Not when I tell you that he

had always proposed to devote his whole life, himself and all he had, to his work, and to keep free of all earthly ties, that he might be able to do it the better? Ought he to have broken through such a resolution as that for me, or for any one?"

"Maybe not. Yet I am sure now that part of what I saw in his face the other day was self-reproach."

"You are mistaken," Lucy answered proudly. "He knew he was doing right." Then, with a swift change of manner: "Muriel, did he send me no message—nothing at all?"

And Muriel repeated all that Philip Irvine had said, and gave the only message he had dared to send.

When all was told, Lucy sat silent for a minute, and let fall two or three quiet tears. "It is a great comfort," she said at last; "it seems sent to me like God-speed for my voyage, doesn't it? If I should never come back, Muriel, you will thank him for that blessing, and tell him how happy it made me, won't you? For"—as she saw her sister shiver slightly—"we must face that possibility, you know. Perhaps I shall not live very long in India, and there would be no harm in giving him such a message then."

"You speak as if his message were of more consequence than your life," Muriel broke out in irrepressible pain. "Do you wish not to get well, Lucy, that you talk like this?"

"I hardly know what I wish sometimes," the girl answered gently.

"At least you might wish to live for the sake of others," Muriel urged passionately. "Even for his sake—Philip Irvine's. If you love him, you would surely wish to spare him such grief."

"Perhaps," said Lucy slowly, "it would not grieve him so much, after all. Not because he does not love me—oh no—but just because he does. I can do so little good, I am of so little account in the world at the best of times; and since I grew weak and ill, I am nothing but a care. I dare say he imagines me suffering, suffering very likely a great deal more than I really do, and unhappy as well; I think sometimes he would be better content if he knew I was safely out of it all."

To hear Lucy talk, it was difficult to believe that she had not seen or heard from her lover for more than three years past. In her implicit trust and intuitive sympathy, she spoke as if she had not been parted from him for a day.

"It is different in his case," she went on

reflectively. "I could not wish him to die before his time; there is so much work to be done, and so few like him to do it. And then, when I think of his hard, lonely life "—the weak voice faltered for the first time—" still I try always to remember that the very hardness and loneliness is only adding brightness to the crown he will have by-and-by."

Almost too deeply moved for words, Muriel bent over Lucy and kissed her forehead. "My darling!" she murmured softly. "Have you been very unhappy all this time, Lucy?"

"Not all the time. At first, when it was quite new and fresh; and afterwards, from time to time—even now occasionally, when I grow foolish and impatient, because I cannot see him or hear of him; but I have so much to comfort me. It is not as if I had really lost him, when I know that he only gave me up for the greater love of God and God's work. Is not that something to be glad of?"

"Yes," Muriel said. "You may well be glad of it."

"Then if I do hear a stray mention of him, it always relates to some good cause which he is helping forward, or some wrong which he is trying to redress, or else to the poor and wretched people whom he is teaching to lead new lives by giving up his own to them; so that I know, as well as if I were with him, that every year he is only growing better, and nobler, and more Christ-like. Dear Muriel"—as her sister bent her head upon her hands—"don't grieve for me so much. Indeed I am not unhappy; you need not be so sorry for me."

Muriel lifted her pale, tearless face. "Sorry for you?" she exclaimed. "If you only knew how I envy you! Lucy, I think you are the happiest woman I ever knew."

CHAPTER III.

"ET TU, BRUTE?"

"There, where I have garner'd up my heart;
Where either I must live, or bear no life,—
To be discarded thence!"

SHAKESPEARE.

"MARGARET," said Paul Wentworth, coming into his sister's morning-room one bleak forenoon early in the following March, "I want you to do me a favour."

"Well, Paul?"

"I am going down to the Delameres' this afternoon for two or three days. Will you have the children here while I am away; or rather, will you have Stella?"

"I will have both gladly," said Margaret, rising from her writing-table. "But why Stella in particular?"

"I am rather uneasy about her," Wentworth answered, knitting his brows and pressing his lips tightly together—a favourite trick of his when anything was weighing on his mind. "She is not like herself."

"Not ill?" inquired his sister eagerly.

"How am I to tell?"—with a sort of suppressed irritability which was, as Margaret well knew, merely a cover for intense and painful anxiety. "She declares there is nothing the matter with her. When I suggested asking Falconer to have a look at her, there was a storm of tears and entreaties, and protestations that she was perfectly well. I did not like to insist, as there really seemed nothing to take hold of, and the bare idea distressed her so much. I don't know why she should have taken such a dislike to poor Falconer, I am sure; he used to be rather a favourite of hers."

"If I had been you, I think I should have insisted."

"You would not if you had seen her just then. I don't know what harm insistance might not have done; she was not fit to be reasoned with."

("Whose fault is it that she is so often unreasonable?" thought Margaret to herself.) Aloud she only asked, "Do you think she has been working too hard at her lessons? I have

noticed myself that she has often seemed depressed and absent of late."

Wentworth turned pale. " You have noticed
it too ?   Since when ? " he demanded in his most
abrupt tone, the tone which with him always
betrayed the strongest mental agitation.

" I can hardly tell.   You see, she comes here
so often that it is almost as if we lived in the
same house ; and when one sees a person daily,
one is slow to notice little changes."

" So it seems," Wentworth observed drily.   " I
suppose you can tell whether the alteration
began days or weeks ago, at any rate ?   Because
that would make a good deal of difference in my
feeling as to consulting some one about her," he
added more gently.

" It is rather weeks than days since I first
thought her out of sorts," Margaret admitted
reluctantly.   " You have not seen it so long, I
suppose ? "

" No, only for about a fortnight past.   She is
curiously changeable : one moment in feverish
spirits, and the next moping and silent.   Mabel
says she is always talking and crying in her
sleep ; and nervous she certainly is.   This very
morning I went suddenly into the schoolroom
before going out, and found her there alone—

at her prayers, I verily believe, for she sprang
off her knees looking guilty and distressed, dear
child! as if she had been caught doing something wrong. Well, the mere surprise of my
unexpected entry brought on an attack of such
violent trembling that I was quite alarmed.
There must be something wrong, Margaret."

" She never used to be nervous," said Margaret
reflectively. "I really think she must have been
overdoing her brain in some way."

"I don't fancy so. Miss Lawson is very
judicious ; common sense is her strongest point,
and I know exactly the amount of work she
gives the girls. It is not too great for any
healthy child of Stella's age."

Silence for a minute. Then Wentworth added,
with a manifestly painful effort, "The worst of
it all is that Stella has grown very reserved.
She does not talk to me in the same perfectly
frank way that she used to do. I cannot feel
sure that she is not suffering, and won't acknowledge it."

Margaret's expression became grave. "And
you want me to inquire into things for you, and
find out if there is anything really amiss, while
Stella is here? Is that it?" she asked in a
business-like manner.

Wentworth winced. He hated admitting that any one might possibly succeed with his idol, where he himself had failed.

"Good heavens, no!" he replied hotly. "The last thing I wish is to have the child tormented with questionings and catechizings, which would only induce her to think herself seriously ill when probably there is nothing in the world the matter with her. I merely want you to have her with you while I am gone, and just observe her quietly. Surely any woman worth the name could do such a simple thing as that! If you think she needs doctoring, take her to some man who knows what he is about—not Falconer, as she has taken such an invincible dislike to him—and write to me at once what he says. Do you understand?"

Margaret rejoined meekly that she thought she quite understood. She was a spirited woman enough on ordinary occasions, but she did not often venture on a dispute with her half-brother, especially when he was in a dictatorial mood. Besides, she was sufficiently sorry for his present anxiety to overlook easily any little want of fraternal politeness on his part.

Wentworth, after bidding his sister good-bye, and executing two or three little matters of

rather pressing business, went on his way homeward considerably lighter in heart for having
enlisted Margaret's aid. He was to leave Paddington by the three o'clock express that day,
and it was now already past two, so he had little
time to spare. Of his younger daughter, who
was spending the afternoon with some youthful
friends, he had already taken leave; there remained only his farewells to Stella. And Stella
he found, not as formerly he would have done,
ready to waylay him on the stairs or curled up
reading in his study armchair, but sitting solitary
in a window-seat of the deserted schoolroom—
for it was holiday-time, and Miss Lawson was
temporarily absent from her unruly kingdom—
with a countenance showing unmistakable traces
of recent tears. She looked up, on her father's
entrance, with one of those nervous starts which
were becoming habitual to her.

"Well, little one," said Wentworth, sitting
down on the window-seat likewise, and putting
a caressing arm about her, "I have arranged
for you to go over to —— Street till Friday
But why are you sitting up here in this forlorn
condition? And you have been crying again!
This is terrible, my darling; there must be
something quite amiss with you."

Stella uttered an incoherent murmur to the effect that there was nothing the matter with her; she was not ill.

"No," said Wentworth incisively, a new light seeming to break in upon his mind, "I don't believe you are ill, my child; I think you are unhappy." He looked searchingly into her eyes. "I see I am right, dear; what is it?"

Stella made a sudden movement which had the effect of half hiding her face on her father's shoulder. Except by that significant action, she returned no answer to his question.

"There is something pressing on your mind, my star," Wentworth went on, stroking her hair with a kind of wistful tenderness. "This is the very first time you have ever kept any of your troubles from me, and see how you are punished, properly punished, by your conscience for your undutiful behaviour! Come, confess."

He felt her quiver in his arms before she answered desperately: "I can't! I would if I could—do believe me, father! But I can't, I can't!"

"We will see about that," Wentworth rejoined —very gravely, but very lovingly as well. "I do not choose that you should keep this trouble of yours, whatever it may be, secret from me,

Stella. I don't often order you to do things, my little girl; but for this once I speak with authority. Tell me immediately what is the matter."

Stella did not stir. She only murmured again, "I can't!" in a voice which sounded rebellious to Wentworth's ear.

"You refuse to tell me?" he exclaimed in amazement, incensed at last, but sorely wounded as well. "Then you cannot be surprised if I conclude that it is something more than a childish scrape which is weighing on your spirits. For the first time in your life, I am seriously angry with you, Stella. You have offended me deeply. What have I done? How have I ever failed in love towards you, that you should deny me your confidence in this way?"

The accent of pathetic reproach in his last words almost nullified the severity of those which had preceded them. It went straight to Estelle's heart.

"Can't you believe me?" she cried, in piteous pleading, springing upright and standing before him. "I cannot tell you; I dare not tell you! I have done nothing wrong; it was not my fault. Won't you trust me a little, father? I am not such a child now; won't you believe that I may be doing right in not telling ? And I have promised too," she added half to herself.

But Wentworth's quick ear had caught the last faint sentence. "Promised!" he repeated sharply. "Promised that you would keep a secret, some secret that you are ashamed of, from me! What right had you to make such a promise? If you have done so, then I absolve you from it; and that is enough."

"It is not enough," cried Stella, standing at bay. "I won't break it." Her voice sank suddenly to a tone of entreaty again, and the great dark eyes filled with tears. "Don't look at me like that, please, father darling; I promised for your sake."

"Don't equivocate!" Wentworth interrupted, with an ominous flash in his eyes. He was thoroughly roused now. "How could you have promised to deceive me *for my sake?* To whom did you give this promise, pray? To Mabel, I suppose?"

"Oh no! Mab does not know. I would never have let her know."

Wentworth regarded his daughter curiously. "I am glad to hear it," he remarked. "I should be sorry to think that my children were in league to deceive me. Now, Stella, for the last time, will you tell me the truth?"

"How can I?" she asked, with a look of anguish, and of intense effort to master that anguish, quite terrible to see on so young a face. "I could not, even if I had not promised her."

"Of whom are you speaking?" demanded Wentworth sternly. "Who is it that knows this secret of yours?"

Stella buried her face in her hands. "Oh, I hope I am doing right to tell," she sobbed. "Mrs. Arlingham knows; I promised Mrs. Arlingham."

Perhaps it was as well that she could not see her father's face at that moment.

"Is that all?" he asked presently, in a constrained voice. "Is there no one else?"

"No one. Only Mrs. Arlingham."

"And Mrs. Arlingham advised you to keep this secret from me? That was a strange thing for Mrs. Arlingham to do," Wentworth observed. "Why did you make her the keeper of your secrets, may I ask?"

"Because I could not help it, and——"

A rattle of the door handle, and a prolonged and respectful fit of coughing from the footman. "The brougham's at the door, sir; and there is barely time to catch the express, if you please." Having delivered himself of this warning announcement, John Thomas withdrew with all convenient speed, perceiving his presence to be neither necessary nor desirable just then.

Wentworth got up and buttoned his overcoat. Then he turned again to his daughter.

"Have you nothing more to say, Stella ? Are you content to let me go away like this ?"

Stella threw herself impulsively into his arms, and clung about his neck. "I am not content; it breaks my heart," she said. "It is not that I will not tell you, father; I cannot. And though you don't believe me, it is for your sake."

At her last words—words which to him seemed manifestly false—Wentworth stiffened into stone. "You will not very easily persuade me of that," he replied. "Perhaps when I come back, you will be able to make up your mind to tell the truth, also for my sake. I assure you I should much prefer it to anything else you could do for me. Meanwhile, good-bye."

And he started on his journey looking even a trifle more self-reliant and impassive than usual, but with a tempest of anger and wounded love raging in his heart, and an unutterable anguish of keen-edged disappointment stabbing him through and through. Anger was uppermost, perhaps, for the moment. He did well to be angry, he told himself.

Yet what did it all mean—this mysterious reserve of Stella's, this still more mysterious action of Muriel's in the background? Why was fate always at work forging fresh links to draw him close to this woman, whom, for the very reason that he loved her so passionately, he had honestly striven to renounce? What did it mean? And as he asked himself again and again this fruitless question, there came to him in every sound—in the sighing of the wind, in the irregular patter of the raindrops against the carriage-window, even in the measured and constant forward motion of the train itself—the same unvarying answer, which to his excited imagination carried fiendish mockery in its unchanging syllables, "*Mrs. Arlingham knows.*"

CHAPTER IV.

WHAT MRS. ARLINGHAM KNEW.

"There's rue for you; and here's some for me—you may wear your rue with a difference."—SHAKESPEARE.

PAUL WENTWORTH prolonged his stay in the country considerably beyond the two or three days he had originally allowed himself. There was no temptation to return to town during the recess, and even when Parliament reassembled there was very little doing at first. Easter fell early that year, and people seemed inclined to linger on as late as possible at their country houses, and were only too glad to welcome Wentworth among their guests; so he paid a number of short visits to various acquaintances in the home counties, intending to wind up his holiday with a couple of nights at Graymere, Lord Carlton's pretty little retreat near Marlow.

He had partially recovered the shock of his

last interview with his daughter, but only
partially. That is to say, the first fever-heat of
his indignation had cooled somewhat, but the
wound inflicted by Stella's hand still throbbed
painfully. She had sent after him a letter,
pathetic in its unstudied distress, entreating his
forbearance and forgiveness; and he had written
a tender and reassuring reply. It was impossible
for him to cherish abiding anger against his idol.
But nevertheless, he could not forget that to his
appeals for perfect frankness Stella had shown
herself as obdurate as ever. She would give no
hint as to the cause of that nameless trouble
which had erected itself into a barrier between
them, and met all arguments on the subject by
a stubborn silence which filled Wentworth with
mingled anxiety and impatience. The old perfect confidence was gone for ever.

Yet Margaret wrote encouragingly, endeavouring to convince her brother that only some
girlish fancifulness was in question, and assuring
him that Stella herself was clearly making great
and generally successful efforts to throw off her
inexplicable fits of depression. The physician to
whom Margaret had taken her said there was
nothing seriously amiss: "a little want of tone,
and perhaps rather too active a brain at work."

He had recommended fresh air and tonics, and fewer lessons for the present; all of which recommendations Margaret was carrying out to the letter, and, she thought, with beneficial results.

So Wentworth tried to persuade himself that he was satisfied, remaining all the while profoundly anxious. But as nothing could really relieve his anxiety short of learning Stella's secret, either from herself or from the only person besides herself who knew it, and both these alternatives appeared for the present alike out of the question, he tried to thrust aside all further speculations on the subject, and roused himself to meet his old friends, the Carltons, with such spirits as he could command.

He arrived rather early in the afternoon, and found only his hostess within-doors. All the men belonging to the house-party had gone to a distant meet of the Buckhounds, and the ladies were out walking. When Lady Carlton had welcomed her guest, she proposed, if he were not tired by his journey, to go and meet them. " I know which way my niece will have taken," she said, " and I have not been out yet myself to-day, so I shall be glad of a little fresh air, if you feel inclined for a stroll." Wentworth felt very much inclined that way, after a tedious journey in a particularly crowded and stifling railway-carriage.

It was a pleasant spring afternoon, and Lady Carlton herself an agreeable and appreciative companion, so that Wentworth was rather sorry when, after half an hour's leisurely walking, he descried the company they had come to meet—four or five more or less youthful feminine figures, amongst which towered conspicuously the tall form of Lady Carlton's niece, a handsome, majestic young matron of eight or nine and twenty. Wentworth knew her slightly, and advanced to greet her, while Lady Carlton proceeded to introduce him to the rest, who were all strangers to him. No, not all; or else why this fierce painful thrill at his heart, why this wild throbbing of his pulses at sight of the girlish figure in the grey dress a little further on ? By an instinctive, involuntary movement, Muriel Arlingham had turned aside, apparently searching for primroses in the picturesque overgrown hedgerow; but in a moment more she had recovered herself, and came forward, her pale face looking very pure and proud under her wide grey hat with its drooping feathers.

"How do you do, Mr. Wentworth?" she said in a soft even voice. "You have brought us fine weather, I am glad to see. This is the first really spring day we have had this year."

He made some light response as his hand touched hers, and then every one else began to talk too. It was not such a terrible affair, this meeting, after all.

They all turned and walked back together towards the house. Wentworth was a little more silent than his wont, perhaps; but Muriel talked fluently. Some of her companions questioned her about a visit she had paid to Rome during the previous winter, and she expatiated enthusiastically on its delights.

"I wonder you enjoyed it so much," Lady Carlton's niece, Mrs. Bernard, observed at last. "You were so unwell when you were there; I remember I thought you looking deplorable when we passed through. I came home feeling quite anxious about her, didn't I, Aunt Mary? I don't believe Rome agreed with you, but I suppose you rose superior to all that. Now, if the climate of a place doesn't suit me, I always hate the place."

"Oh, I felt the drawbacks to Rome at the time," Muriel answered lightly, " but now I have forgotten them, and only remember the advantages. It is a way one has in looking back on past pleasures, don't you think? The little anxieties, the little rubs, the little annoyances—one forgets all these, and recollects only the broad general happiness, which at the time, perhaps, they may have marred considerably."

"So that, after all, happiness always seems greater in retrospect than it ever was in actual possession? Is that your experience?" asked Lady Carlton, smiling.

"I think so, on the whole," Muriel replied, trying to smile also.

"What do you make, then, of the poet's ' sorrow's crown of sorrow'?" Wentworth asked suddenly. "When the very thought of the lost happiness has grown hateful, for instance?"

"It need never become so, according to my ideas," Muriel answered in an unruffled tone, as if she were discussing some purely academic question. "I am at issue with the poet on that point, though he is the divine poet. Lady Carlton, you have a brier on your dress; let me take it off for you."

Wentworth walked on with his hostess after that, and paid no further attention to Mrs. Arlingham's movements, until they reached the gate leading from the meadows through which they had been wandering to the shrubberies of

Graymere, and he discovered that she was no longer of the party. Then he asked where she was.

"I think she stopped to speak to an old woman near the last stile," said Mrs. Bernard.

"We will wait for her here, then," Lady Carlton said. "It was old Jane Townsend she spoke to, probably; Jane is a great crony of Mrs. Arlingham's."

"If that is the case, their conversation may be of a protracted nature, perhaps, unless it is interrupted," Wentworth remarked. "Suppose I go and interrupt it?"

He started swiftly across the field, with a sudden eager purpose fermenting in his brain. Why, since chance or Providence had thrown Muriel in his way again, should he not try through her to fathom the mystery of Stella's trouble? What if she did resent his appeal? He could but make the attempt; and for the moment Muriel herself was not so much the woman he loved as the holder of his child's secret.

When he reached her she was just taking leave of her humble friend, an ancient dame who moved feebly and with difficulty with the help of a stout stick, but whose bright grey eyes

and wrinkled countenance still beamed with
intelligence.

"Then Lizzie is no better?" Muriel was saying, as she took the old woman's hand.

"No, noways better."

"Does she still suffer very much?"

"Above a bit. But she be rare and patient.
'Mother,' says she to me, 'I'd rather take my
punishment in this life than in the life to come.'
And I reckon she's right. Our sins be bound to
find us out some time, here or there."

"But there is forgiveness for those," Muriel
murmured shyly, flushing as she perceived Wentworth standing near.

"So there be, so there be—for the sins themselves. But there's the consequences, my dear
lady; we can't undo them—leastways, not here.
I reckon, perhaps, never. I mean no disrespect
to the Almighty, but it seems as if the Lord
Himself couldn't undo that as is done. And so
I take it we must be punished some time; and
better here, as poor Lizzie says, comforting herself like. I'll be sure and give her your message,
ma'am, thank you kindly. Good evening, ma'am."
And the aged creature hobbled away, with a
glance of admiring affection at Muriel, and one
of half-distrustful inquiry at the man who had

stood silently by to listen to the outpourings of her simple soul.

"Is that scientific theology or unscientific heresy?" he asked, with the old scornful curl of the lip, as he and Muriel moved forward in the direction of Lady Carlton and her friends.

"It is too terrible to be treated lightly, anyway," Muriel answered. "And I think it is terribly true, myself."

He looked at her curiously. "I thought you good people professed a religion of love," he remarked half mockingly, yet with a questioning sound in his voice.

Muriel returned his look steadfastly, and there seemed to him a sort of compassion in her gaze. "I can only answer you in Browning's words," she said—"'All's Love, but all's Law.' At least, so it seems to me."

"You think so?" he rejoined, and then they walked on faster, and said no more.

They were nearing the shrubbery gate, and he had spoken no word on the subject which lay nearest his heart, when Muriel herself unconsciously gave him the required opening. "How are your children?" she asked, chiefly to break the awkward silence.

"They are very well," he answered. "At

least, Mabel is. I am a little anxious about
Stella."

"About Stella?" Muriel repeated with a
startled look.

"Yes. I wanted to speak to you about her.
Will you give me a few minutes alone to do so,
either to-day or to-morrow?"

"You wish to speak to me about Stella?"

"About her, and her only," he replied impatiently. "You need not fear," he added, lower-
ing his voice, for they were now almost within
earshot of the rest of the party, "that I shall
trouble you with my own concerns, or with any
subject whatever other than a secret of my
daughter's, of which she tells me you have the
keeping. I think I may fairly claim the right
to inquire into this. When can I see you in
private?"

Strange to say, Muriel showed no resentment
at Wentworth's imperious manner. She merely
answered in the same subdued tone that he had
used, "You will find me in the library half an
hour before dinner." Then they came up with
Lady Carlton, and nothing further could be said.

Wentworth ensconced himself in the empty
library—safe to remain untenanted for the next
half-hour—as soon as the first bell had rung and

dispersed the other guests to their rooms; nor had he long to wait for Muriel's promised appearance. In about five minutes she came quietly in. She was dressed in black, and there seemed to Wentworth something strange and unusual, yet beautiful with an almost unearthly beauty, in the expression of her face. Was it patience he read there, or pity? He could not feel sure.

"This is very kind of you," he said briefly, and would have placed a chair for her. But she declined it with a gesture of thanks, and, murmuring something about the coldness of the evening, moved to the mantelpiece and stood leaning against it, holding out her slender hands to the blaze of the newly kindled wood fire. She did seem really cold, for she shivered from time to time.

"You wished to ask me a question?" she said at last, seeing that Wentworth, usually so fluent, forbore to begin the conversation, and remained at the other end of the hearthrug in embarrassed silence. "A question relating to your daughter Stella?"

He bent his head in assent. "Just so. For some time past I have been uneasy about Stella, Mrs. Arlingham. She has been quite unlike herself; moody, depressed, changeable, and—

what she never was in her life before—extremely reserved. Neither her aunt, her sister, nor I myself can induce her to tell us what it is that weighs on her spirits."

He paused for a rejoinder; then, receiving none, went on : " You can imagine that all this makes me very anxious—the more that I find the child is not ill physically, so that I am driven to conclude she has some trouble of mind. Indeed, she has admitted as much to me. It is the only thing I have induced her to admit," he added with great bitterness; "for I find that she has been taught it is her duty to keep her trouble a secret from me, and so well has she learnt her lesson, that all my arguments are powerless to shake her determination. I own I am surprised to find, further, that her adviser in this matter is yourself."

No answer issued from Muriel's lips; but in the grey twilight which was beginning to fill the room, as the sun set behind the trees that shaded its single window, Wentworth saw her tremble and change colour.

"I have lost my daughter's confidence, it seems," he continued more bitterly still, " and, as I gather from her, in consequence of your instructions. I have never extenuated my

offences against you, or pretended to be any
better than I am—which, God knows, is bad
enough—but could not you have chosen some
other means of wreaking your just vengeance
on me? Whatever else I have been, my children
have not found me wanting; there at least my
conscience acquits me. Could not you, in your
merciless saintliness, have devised some other
punishment for me than this one?"

Muriel uttered a low, inarticulate exclamation.
"Do you mean to say that you believe I did this
thing willingly?" she demanded. "Or what is
it you think I have done, except it were to try
and save you and her both in so far as I could?
What has Stella told you?"

"She has told me that she cannot explain the
reason of her trouble because she has promised
not to do so—because she has promised you. 'I
promised Mrs. Arlingham; and Mrs. Arlingham
knows'"—dwelling with marked emphasis on
the words which had been haunting him so
cruelly for weeks past. "Therefore, since you
do know, Mrs. Arlingham, I have to beg that
you will impart your knowledge to me. What
is wrong with my Stella?"

There was a sudden pathetic break, a sudden
tender inflection in his voice at the final question.

"Don't ask!" Muriel entreated, leaning forward with a gesture of supplication. "As you value your own happiness and hers, don't ask! Believe me, it is better not, a thousand times better. She will forget it, outgrow it, live it down, and you need never know. I believe she is strong enough to go on now as she has begun. For your own sake, above all, I entreat you to spare yourself while it is still possible."

Wentworth was ashen-grey by now, but his mouth was set in a firm uncompromising line. "I thank you, I have no desire to spare myself," he replied. "I am not so easily moved as you imagine; and when my daughter's happiness is at stake, I prefer shattering my own sensitive feelings to being kept in the dark respecting hers. May I again request you to tell me all you know?"

Muriel drew a long breath, as of one about to make some superhuman effort. "I will," she answered, and moved a little from the mantelpiece, leaning both hands on the back of a chair standing near.

"Last January," she began, fixing her eyes mechanically on Wentworth's face, like a child repeating its lesson, "before we went to Rome, I went up to London for a couple of days. I called to see your sister Margaret. Your children were with her; it was Stella's birthday. Margaret was suffering from neuralgia, and could not go out."

"Well?" said Wentworth, more gently than he had spoken yet.

"Mabel was to have gone that day to the dentist's in Wimpole Street, and Margaret was distressed at not being able to take her. She asked me to go in her stead, and I consented. Stella begged to go with us."

Again Muriel had to pause to take breath. She was panting audibly now, and where Wentworth stood he could almost fancy he heard the beating of her heart.

"I left Stella by herself in the outer room at Mr. Campbell's," she went on, quivering from head to foot, "with the *Graphic* to look over while we were gone. I thought we should not be away long; but Mabel was very nervous, and we were detained longer than I had expected. When I came out again, I saw by Stella's face what had happened. She had read it all."

"Read what?" Wentworth demanded hoarsely.

"She had got hold of a number of *Town Talk*."

"Not the one—not that of the 20th of January?"

" Yes. That one."

" Oh, my God !" And with that one exceeding bitter cry Paul Wentworth turned and flung his head down upon the mantelpiece, and covered his face with his hands. And for the space of a few minutes there was a terrible silence.

At length Wentworth lifted his head. " I ask your pardon," he said faintly, " for whatever I said in my haste just now. I suppose the presentiment of this thing was upon me. Did she show you what she had read ? "

" Yes. It was the first I knew of the existence of that paragraph, or I would have died rather than have left her within reach of it."

" Perhaps you believed the story it told of me ? Many people did, in spite of its inherent improbabilities. When my best friend's wife left her home suddenly and without explanation, it was of course quite natural to conclude that *I* was in some way responsible for the step."

" I did not believe a word of the story. It was manifestly an invention, as I told Stella."

Hitherto Wentworth had spoken without looking round ; now he turned his haggard face towards Muriel. " I am surprised at your feeling able to disbelieve the charge—until it was withdrawn. What did you say besides to—to *her ?* "

"I told her to forget the whole thing; to put it from her mind; to regard it as springing out of that bitter political jealousy which delights in slandering its opponents, and never to think of it again. Then——"

"Go on," he said sternly.

"She referred to the comments that followed the story—to those references to the past. She asked me if it were true that such things were said in the world; if people really thought of—of you as *Town Talk* said they did? She seemed almost beside herself at the idea."

"And you said?"

"I told her that—like most prominent public men—you had your share of enemies, and that some of these were unscrupulous men, always ready to magnify or invent a fault. I begged her not to dwell on anything they might say, and she answered, 'It cannot matter if it is not true.'"

"Was that all? It could hardly have ended there."

"No, it was not all," Muriel answered with quivering lips. "I thought I had pacified her, and put her off—that all might still be well— when all at once she caught my hands and said, 'After all, this is the real question: is it true,

any of it ? I want only one word.' Mr. Wentworth, I did my best—Heaven knows I did—
for her and for—for you. But it was useless.
She put aside what I said, she divined everything I would not say. She forbade me to play
with her; she wanted only to know the truth.
' Was it true, any of it ?' For pity's sake, don't
ask me to tell you any more ! "

"I think," he said very quietly, "I can imagine
the rest for myself. Don't distress yourself, Mrs.
Arlingham; I am quite convinced you did your
best. Truth will out, you know, sooner or later,
and even if you had been a better actress, Stella
could easily have got her question answered elsewhere. The verification of *Town Talk's* references would have been a matter of no difficulty
for any one—in any case, the wreck of her faith
in me was inevitable. The paragraph itself
would have done the work unaided, in the end."

"At least it could not kill her love," Muriel
said tremulously. "Do not imagine that."

"I don't imagine it for a moment. If she had
ceased to care for me, I could hardly have broken
her heart."

"Surely, surely," Muriel pleaded, "it is not so
bad as that. She has suffered very much, no
doubt—oh, I know it; I can guess something of

what she has felt since that day—but part of her suffering is due to the consciousness of the secret that has thrust itself between you and her. Blame me for that. But for me she might have been frank with you from the first. But I thought too much of you, too little of her, and so I laid on her a burden too heavy for her child's strength. Now that you know everything, it is in your power to take that burden away."

"And when I *have* taken it away—what then?" he asked. "Can I take away the knowledge of evil, too—an evil of which she was wholly ignorant till she learnt it by the recital of my sins? Can I take away the shame—O God, *mine!*—which has crushed her innocent spirits, and made her afraid to lift her eyes in my presence for fear I should read my condemnation in them?"

"Sometimes I think," Muriel murmured, flushing deep crimson as she spoke, "that even now the whole meaning of those—those accusations can hardly have revealed itself to her. Much must have remained vague."

"Perhaps so, for a while. But all was not vague, and what was unmistakable would soon help her to interpret the rest. Besides, she is fast growing into a woman : will you guarantee me against the further experience of life which must infallibly teach her all that remains for her to learn of the meaning of that accursed paragraph? No, there is no escaping this thing, no possibility of rendering it less horrible. Your old crone was right, Mrs. Arlingham. One's deeds and their consequences remain, and the Almighty Himself cannot do away with either—even were I so presumptuous as to expect Him to interfere on my behalf.

"Well," he added, after a moment, "I wonder you don't remind me that I only reap as I have sown. I am quite ready to acknowledge it myself. 'All's Love, but all's Law,' you said this afternoon, I remember. I see the law here most distinctly; I cannot say I perceive much of the other thing. Why, if Providence was determined to punish me, could it not do so without involving that innocent child? Some lesser torture might have sufficed even for me, one would think. If I have been all that my worst enemies say, am I to blame for the deadly mistake that poisoned my life from the very outset, and made me what I am? I do not expect you to understand me. How should you? To do that, you must know what it is to have the love of your life turned into a veritable curse, to have your dearest faith trampled in the dust, and your whole existence darkened by a deception so bitter that it has destroyed the best part of your belief in human nature itself. Since you do not know this——"

"Do not I know it?" The words broke from Muriel against her will.

A change passed over Wentworth's face. "You, too!" he exclaimed. "Not—— Muriel! Is this what I have done for you?"

She hesitated a moment. Then she put aside conventionality, reticence, pride, fear, and took up the task she deemed assigned her.

"I did not mean to have said it," she replied; "but I will not take back my words now. That is what you did for me once."

"So," he answered, "I have succeeded in ruining the lives of the two I love best in the world. Truly, my punishment is well devised."

"My life is not ruined," said Muriel quietly. "It never can be, except by my own fault."

"As mine has been."

"As yours is not," she contradicted gently. "Gone very much astray, perhaps; defaced and spoilt for what it might have been once, but surely not past repair. I, too, went wholly wrong, yet——"

"My sins and yours!" he interrupted, with

a half-smile terrible in its contemptuous self-mockery. " They are so alike ! "

" When weighed against our different temptations—who knows ? " she asked. " It would have been easy for me to do right, compara-. tively; perhaps it was hard for you."

His eyes softened almost reverentially. " I cannot see where you failed," he said. " First in your early childhood, and now, even as the wife of a man who does not love you—— " He set his teeth fiercely.

" No, he does not love me," she answered with a sad humility. " Have I any right to expect that he should ? I have done him a great wrong, for I married him without loving him. I married him, though—— "

" You loved me," Wentworth put in, in a quiet, matter-of-fact way.

Muriel flushed again, a painful, burning flush " I persuaded myself at the time that it was no so. I deceived myself, to begin with; deceived myself wilfully. I was impatient, and wanted to forget, and my pride had been wounded—it does not matter how. I thought my marriage would help me there. I was vain, too, and liked power; and it was pleasant to be loved—so I thought." She stopped, with tears in her voice.

"When I first saw that I was nothing to my husband," she resumed, "I was angry, bitterly angry. 'Why should everything fail me like this?' I thought. And when you came back and roused the old pain again, I was angry too. It seemed so hard that I could never be left in peace; that I must be always suffering like this. But at last I have learnt why it is, or I am at least learning. And so my life is not ruined, and yours need not be."

"What analogy can possibly exist in such a case?" Wentworth retorted. "You have not brought misery on others. There are no hopeless consequences of evil-doing for you to contemplate."

"You are mistaken," Muriel replied; "I can never undo the evil of my marriage. How do I know but what, if Jack had had for his wife a woman who really loved him, instead of one like me"—she drooped her head heavily—"perpetually fighting with her own false heart, he might not have been a wholly different man? That thought is almost more than I can bear. Yet it is exactly that which I must learn to bear: that, and the loss of his regard, which is a daily trouble and grief to me—all the more because I know it is just that I should have lost it— what

can I do but take it as patiently as I can?
Even"—and here she grew white to the lips—
"that love for you which I cannot wholly root
out—I think sometimes that the pain and the
shame of it will stay with me all my life as part
of my punishment; and all that is left to me is
to bear them as such."

Her tears were almost choking her, but she
wrestled them down and went on.   "Yet I don't
despair.   It is better to feel as I do now, than to
be—as I was for a time—so hard that one can
feel nothing.   You will wonder why I have told
you all this," she concluded hurriedly.

"No," Wentworth answered, still with that
fixed reverential gaze, "I don't wonder.   I
know; I understand perfectly.   You would
shrink from nothing if you could save me, as you
think.   To help me in my bitter strait, you do
not even hesitate to step down from your own
pure safe elevation and to put yourself on a level
with *me!*   You angel!   But I am past your
help now.   Since I have no longer even my
children to live better for, what matter what the
end of it all is?"

"This is not an end, but a beginning," Muriel
said.

"A beginning!" he repeated ironically.   "A

beginning, verily! out of such intolerable shame
and horror as this!" She saw him clench his
hand and turn away to conceal the spasm of
pain which shook his features. "When I have
just become utterly hateful to myself, and loathe
my own existence! Besides, who told you I
had any desire for such a beginning? Will
it give me back that child's love and trust—the
only thing, except one, in this world that I really
prized and valued, and would have given my
life for, gladly? Forgive me, though; I have no
right to inflict my railings upon you. Can you
forgive me for the sake of that which I may not
even speak to you, you for whom it is little to
say I would do anything?"

Muriel's face was transfigured by a sudden
illumination. "Then do the one thing that could
make me happy, even now," she answered. "Be
what God surely meant you to be—the noblest
man I ever knew."

She did not wait for a reply, but before she
could quit the room one reached her, low and
broken indeed, but distinctly audible nevertheless. "Your faith is truly great. If I had not
lost Stella, I almost think——" Wentworth's
voice failed him.

Muriel turned impulsively and stretched out

her hand towards him for an instant; but he made no responsive movement. It was only a slight momentary gesture, quickly withdrawn again, and perhaps from its very slightness and rapidity it passed unnoticed by Wentworth. Or perhaps he did see, and yet purposely ignored it; taking, by that simple act of self-enforced quiescence, the very first step upwards that he had taken for many and many a day.

CHAPTER V.

ART—OR NATURE?

> "If there be
> A devil in man, there is an angel too,
> And if he did that wrong you charge him with,
> His angel broke his heart."
>
> TENNYSON.

How she got through the dinner that followed closely on her interview with Wentworth, or how she bore her part in the long evening which succeeded that, Muriel never had any clear and distinct recollection. She only remembered vaguely that German politics had formed the principal topic of general conversation, and that she had talked a great deal—she imagined, rather more brilliantly than usual; but all her memories of the scene were so nightmare-like and phantasmagoric, and her own condition of mind while the necessary tension lasted seemed to her, on reflection, to have been so strange and so abnormal, that it was almost a relief to wake up on the morrow, after a short morning sleep, to the old, weary, but safe sense of suffering and endurance. Yet the return to her ordinary self made the ordeal of meeting Wentworth again all the more difficult.

It was rather late when she appeared in the breakfast-room, but her first glance round the table showed her that he was not present. Perhaps he was still out on his wanderings: he had a fancy for early morning walks in the country, she knew. Nothing more likely. Yet no: for what was this that Lord Carlton was saying in reply to the lady on his other hand, who had made her entry at the same moment as Mrs. Arlingham ?

"He's gone, I am sorry to say ; gone by the early train, in answer to an urgent summons from his sister. Didn't you hear the stir in the house soon after six this morning ? There was barely time to get him off when the telegram came. It had arrived at the office just too late for sending out last night, unluckily, or he might have caught the night mail, and saved several hours."

"Illness at home, I suppose ?" said Lord Carlton's neighbour. Muriel's lips felt paralyzed.

"Yes, one of his daughters. The eldest, I believe. At least, I think he said it was the eldest. I only saw him for a moment as he was starting. Time was everything to him, for he ought to have had the telegram the day before yesterday; but owing to his not having sent his last two addresses to his sister, or left them where he was staying previously, it has been following him from place to place, and has been telegraphed to at least half a dozen wrong addresses. I trust he may not be too late, for I fear the daughter is very ill."

"Had she met with an accident?"

"I don't know, Mrs. Russell. The telegram was not very explicit, I dare say; telegrams seldom are. But I did not actually see it. I should hardly fancy there had been an accident, however; a sudden illness rather, I think I gathered. Poor Wentworth! it was a terrible shock to him. I think I never saw a man in such a frantic state of anxiety. Of course this unlucky delay made things worse for him."

"His wife died suddenly in his absence from the effects of an accident, I recollect," Mrs. Russell commented reflectively. "Quite a tragical end hers was, poor thing! She was so pretty, too. But she and her husband were not on very

good terms, were they ? People talked a good
deal some years ago. I don't know whose fault
it was, exactly."

Lord Carlton's fine countenance clouded with
annoyance. " Neither do I," he answered stiffly.
" Mr. Wentworth is not a man given to the discussion of his domestic affairs even with his
friends, of whom I am happy to count myself
one." After which remark, the lady deemed it
prudent to try a change of subject, and Lord
Carlton gladly seconded her efforts.

Meanwhile the early train, dragging its slow
parliamentary length along, was just landing
Wentworth at the Great Western terminus in
London. To his fevered impatience—an impatience to which the speed of the fastest
express that ever ran would have seemed halting
—the journey of three hours had been a period
of veritable torture, of momentarily increasing
dread. At intervals he read and re-read the
words of Margaret's telegram, vainly trying to
gather some grain of encouragement from the
message which simply said in its cruel brevity :
" *Stella very ill with sudden inflammation of the
lungs.*" Not a word more. Not even " Come ; "
but then Margaret knew that it was unnecessary
to add that. And two whole days lost already !

He could not, dared not, think what might have happened meanwhile. He should go mad if he did ; he must turn his thoughts elsewhere. He looked resolutely out of the window.

Over Maidenhead Bridge—how large Maidenhead was growing! The place was getting quite spoilt, to Wentworth's mind. These wretched little suburban residences, with their clothes-lines and gravel tennis-courts, were ruining it utterly. Those people in the bigger villa close by the river-arch, which would proudly advertise itself as " standing in its own grounds," no doubt, were playing tennis as usual. Did they never do anything else ? He wondered if they played at night, by moonlight ? Perhaps they were a family of a dozen or so, and took the court by relays. Surely the train was slowing ? Yes, a wayside station. Great heavens ! these stoppages at places where no one ever got in or out! What was the exact hour when Margaret despatched her telegram ? " *April 20th,* 6.25 *a.m.*" Very early. She must have been up all night. That meant it was fully forty-eight hours old before he got it—and forty-eight hours with inflammation of the lungs—— She would think he was staying away deliberately. What marvel, seeing what else she had heard of him ? Supposing—— No, he would not suppose. There was the white country-house, with its sweep of lawn stretching down to the river, and its sweep of woods clothing the hill behind, which he had always admired as a typical specimen of an English home. He speculated idly, as he had speculated many times before, who lived there ? Stella had once said she wished to live there, he remembered. What doctor would Margaret have been likely to call in ? Falconer ? Surely not, after all he had told her himself of Stella's sudden antipathy to Falconer. It would be highly re-prehensible and obstinate of Margaret to have done such a thing; he should have given her credit for more common sense and feeling.

That embankment needed strengthening: there would be a serious landslip in case of heavy rains setting in unexpectedly. The company ought to see to it—he had a great mind to write to the *Times. À propos* of newspapers, there was that letter he had intended to send to the *Morning Planet.* "*Sir—Since you have done me the honour of reporting certain of my more recent utterances in your columns, perhaps you will also be good enough to admit certain corrections of the highly imaginative report which appeared there on Thursday last—corrections trifling in*

themselves, but nevertheless of sufficient im-
portance to contain the whole gist of what I said
—in contradistinction to what your reporter sup-
posed me to say—to the people of Dorchester."
Was that stinging enough? Hardly. These
irresponsible journalists—— And she had held it
in her hand, read it, had it stamped in upon her
memory! It might be haunting her now in the
midst of her pain and her struggle for life; if,
indeed, that struggle were not already over.
What o'clock was it? Only half-past eight.
Only an hour and ten minutes since he left
Graymere? Impossible! And two days lost
already! What could be worse than Margaret's
telegram? If she had only said "ill"—but "very
ill"! What more could she say, except one
thing? Perhaps she had only sent the telegram
to prepare him; perhaps at the very time she
despatched it—— No, no! He would not believe
that. What would Muriel have thought of it?
"I thought too much of you, too little of her."
Well, she must have heard by now. How like
an angel she had looked last night! *"This is not*
an end, but a beginning"—a beginning which
was to end—where? Another station. Only
twenty minutes to nine! and those two days to
make up yet. Why were they stopping this

unconscionable time ? And so on, and so on,
through the three hours which seemed like three
years of an agony long drawn out.

No carriage or servant was awaiting him at
Paddington, but it could not be otherwise, he
remembered, as it was impossible for Margaret
to know when or whence to expect him. This
mattered little; a hansom would take him even
more quickly than his own brougham. Through
noisy, melancholy-looking Cambridge Terrace;
through the network of dull respectable squares
and streets beyond it; then skirting a bit of
Edgware Road, and out into the great stream of
traffic near the Marble Arch ; down Park Lane,
with a glimpse of the bright-hued Park borders
flaunting their full spring glory on his right
hand, and the planes and chestnuts bursting into
tardy, reluctant leaf overhead ; round a familiar
corner, and—— Thank God ! the blinds were up
yet. Till Wentworth saw the open windows he
hardly realized how faint had been his expectation of finding Stella alive.

" Miss Wentworth ? " was the sole question he
put to the elderly butler who answered his
cautious knock. Despite his excitement, he did
not forget that quiet might be needed on entering
the house.

"Much the same, sir, ever since yesterday. She takes a little more notice this morning, so Dickinson says. We expected you yesterday morning, sir."

"I know. The telegram had to follow me about. Is she awake?"

"I expect so, sir. She lies mostly very quiet in the daytime. The doctors are up there now."

Wentworth was half-way across the hall by this time, but turned round to inquire sharply, "What doctors?"

"Dr. Boulton and Sir George Carmichael, sir. Sir George was called in yesterday. Miss Irvine wrote——"

"Where is Miss Irvine?" interrupted Wentworth from the staircase.

"In Miss Wentworth's room, sir."

The door of Stella's room stood wide open—for the day was warm and close, as the later days of April are apt to be occasionally—and from it issued a subdued murmur of voices, the voices of Margaret Irvine and the two physicians, who formed a group just inside the doorway on the right-hand side. On the left, sheltered by the open door itself from view, was Stella's bed, where the girl lay propped up on a great heap of pillows.

She lay very still, as if in a half-stupor of exhaustion. The fever-flush of the past night had already faded from her cheeks, leaving them deadly white; her eyes were closed and her limbs perfectly motionless; but there was a tell-tale line across her smooth young forehead which spoke of semi-conscious pain, and she breathed irregularly and with difficulty. Of the low-voiced questions which Sir George Carmichael was putting to her aunt she seemed totally heedless; but when Wentworth's footfall, guarded as it was, sounded in the corridor, she started slightly, and a shade of colour came into her face. Her eyelids quivered, and finally unclosed.

"Father—it's father," she said in a faint whisper, half to herself. Not so faint, though, but what it caught Wentworth's ear as he crossed the threshold.

He passed by Margaret and the doctors with a curt, unrecognizing nod, and went straight to Stella's bedside, taking the weak hands she tried to hold out to him in his own. "My child, my darling!" he murmured, with what sounded like one great stifled sob. Then he dropped into the vacant chair beside her, and bent his head over the little hands he held.

There was a minute's silence, and Stella gazed

on her father in growing alarm, for he was veri-
fying her worst fears by his strange conduct.
He must, indeed, be angry with her, with an
anger past softening, for he had not even taken
her in his arms or kissed her, his poor sick child!
How could she guess that he dared not; that he
was waiting, in his new-found anguish of humiliation, for a movement from her that she was
powerless to make?

The needful sign came, nevertheless; came in
those irrepressible tears which are only wept of
extreme weakness, and mingled with them the
broken words of appeal: "Father, won't you kiss
me? I am so ill, so ill!"

Wentworth answered nothing. But the em-
brace in which he clasped Stella said more than
any words could have done. She had no need
thenceforward to doubt either his love or his
sorrow.

Not a word was uttered while father and child
thus clung together. Margaret watched them
anxiously, divided between sympathy for her
brother and dismay at the thought of the harm
such agitation as this might effect in a case
like Stella's. Dr. Boulton examined a picture
on the wall, and tapped his foot noiselessly but
impatiently on the carpet with a slightly con-

temptuous expression of countenance; and grey-headed Sir George Carmichael walked across to the window and became lost in contemplation of the hyacinths in the window-box. But he also took off his spectacles, and wiped them significantly more than once.

"Father," Stella whispered, as he held her close, "you are sure you are not angry? Not in the least?"

"Yes, my darling, perfectly sure."

"I was afraid—after what you said. But I meant to do right. If you only knew!"

"I do know," Wentworth said, and then held his breath for the rejoinder.

Stella trembled violently. "How—how did you know?"

"Mrs. Arlingham told me. Hush, darling! it is all no matter. Don't think of it any more."

"No one else ever knew of it," Stella exclaimed excitedly into Wentworth's ear. "Not even Aunt Margaret. Sometimes I was afraid I might have talked of it when I didn't quite know things—at night, you know—but she says I never did, never!"

Wentworth was speechless.

"I was afraid Mabel might guess, too," Stella faltered on, "but she has no idea. Oh, father!

why didn't you come to me sooner? I have been so ill!"

"My star, I only knew it this morning. I had gone far away from the place where you last heard of me, and they had to send—— What is the matter, darling?"

For Stella's eyes had closed again suddenly, and her head was hanging limp and heavy against his shoulder.

Then Margaret came forward. " It is just one of those attacks of faintness which come over her at times," she said in a quiet, practical tone. " Move, Paul, and let me come to her. There, she will be better presently.—It is not often she speaks so much, or even seems to notice fresh people in the room," she added in a rapid *sotto voce* to her brother. " You had better go and talk to Sir George and Dr. Boulton for a while, and leave her to me."

"Yes; pray come," said one of the two physicians, who was leaving the room, whence he was speedily followed by his colleague. And Wentworth went—went obediently and waited patiently till the indispensable ten minutes' consultation had taken place between the medical men, and he could be admitted to hear his sentence, Stella's sentence, from their lips.

He recovered himself when alone with them—
the pride and self-mastery which had forsaken
him utterly in his daughter's presence came back
to him in that of these comparative strangers.
His questions were as clear and searching as if
he had had both men under cross-examination.
Their manner of reply struck him as very dis-
similar. Dr. Boulton, a little, keen, dark man of
middle age, answered briskly, fully, and straight
to the point; while Sir George Carmichael,
whose naturally spare, stooping figure had been
rendered even more bent and shrunken by advancing age, and whose scanty locks were fast
growing white as snow, gave his answers reluctantly, evasively, and always with evident
pain. On one point, the extreme gravity of the
case under discussion, the doctors were plainly
agreed. Only the younger man enunciated his
opinion with an almost brutal frankness, and
the elder with a grave, kindly sympathy which
made the most of every hopeful or encouraging
symptom.

"She has youth on her side, we must remember," Sir George said, with a compassionate
glance through his spectacles at Wentworth.
"Still, there is no use concealing from you that
the attack is a very acute one, and that her

strength has been rapidly, very rapidly, reduced by it. There are various complications present, you see, which may partly account for this rapid reduction of strength. But not entirely."

"Miss Wentworth has evidently a weakly constitution," Dr. Boulton put in incisively. "Yet I believe she has had good health until now, or, at any rate, until quite recently?"

"Perfect health," Wentworth replied. "She has never known a day's illness."

"Such being the case, she should have been better able to throw off an attack of this kind— unless, as I say, there exists some inherent weakness of constitution. Of course there are complications, as Sir George"—with a slight inclination towards that eminent consultant— "has already informed you."

"What complications?"

"A generally weakened state of health, and a highly excitable condition of the brain and nerves; both of which have greatly tended to increase, if not to produce, the fever which is your daughter's most unfavourable symptom. Sir George quite agrees with me here. There has been a certain amount of delirium present every night since I first saw Miss Wentworth three days ago; and there has also been occa-

sional wandering by day. I have employed
opiates, but with little success so far."

"Would anything painful—any trouble or
anxiety pressing upon the mind be likely to
give rise to such symptoms as you have mentioned?" Wentworth might be supposed to be
addressing Dr. Boulton, but he looked at Sir
George Carmichael, and it was Sir George who
answered—

"Very possibly. Can you suggest"—looking
keenly yet kindly into Wentworth's eyes—"any
probable recent irritation of your daughter's
nerves? Any intellectual excitement, or over-
taxing of the brain? For instance, too many
lessons, or too many sensational novels to read?
I questioned her aunt on the subject, and she
seemed inclined to attribute the breakdown in
health and spirits, which, I am given to understand, occurred some weeks before this illness,
to overwork."

"My sister is mistaken," said Wentworth, with
ashen lips. "Overwork has nothing to do with
the matter. I have discovered the real cause."

"And that is?" queried Dr. Boulton. "I half
fancy I have guessed it too," he added in an
undertone, as if communing with himself.

Wentworth gave him one fiery glance and

went on, addressing himself exclusively to Sir
George this time.

"I dare say you know that the society papers
say unpleasant things of me sometimes. Occasionally they are true; generally the reverse.
One such paragraph, which appeared in *Town
Talk* last January, was, most unhappily, seen
and read by my daughter."

"Ah! most unfortunate indeed!" commented
the irrepressible Boulton. Sir George Carmichael said nothing at all.

"I saw soon afterwards," continued Wentworth, "that something was amiss with her,
but she would not confess what it was, to me
or to any one. I only learnt the truth of the
matter last night from a lady who was accidentally present when the paper fell into her
hands. It appears that she then formed an
inflexible resolution to keep her discovery to
herself, in order to—to spare me at all costs."

Sir George Carmichael grasped Wentworth's
hand impulsively. "I thank you a thousand
times for telling us this," he exclaimed; then
returning to his usual quiet manner: "We know
better now what we have to deal with, you see."

"You think, then, that this trouble has had
an injurious effect?" There was such sup-

pressed agony in the tone of the question that
Sir George Carmichael could gladly have caught
Dr. Boulton by the throat for his brisk " Undoubtedly." As Wentworth still looked at him,
he added reluctantly, " To some extent, perhaps;
we can scarcely pronounce positively. The present illness is purely accidental, we must remember; both Dr. Boulton and Miss Irvine tell me
that it can be clearly traced to a severe chill."

" Can anything be done ? "

" To remove the irritant cause, you mean ?
Well, Mr. Wentworth, I would recommend you
to let your daughter know that you are aware
of her secret, and so get her to try and dismiss
it from her mind. There has evidently been,
from Miss Irvine's reports, an effort at self-
repression for some time past; and this is in itself
a strain upon the mind of so very young a girl."

" She knows already that I have heard all
about it."

" Already ? " Dr. Boulton lifted his eyebrows
slightly. " Good, though; you did well to tell
her at once. Miss Irvine stated that when full
consciousness returned after an attack of semi-
delirium, Miss Wentworth frequently inquired
what she had said — evidently showing that
she was afraid of betraying something. This,

and a few words she let drop when not quite herself, first started that guess of mine which has been proved correct."

Wentworth turned quickly away for a moment, and the aspect of his countenance when he turned back again did not dispose Sir George very kindly towards his talkative colleague. But he managed to restrain himself until, after wringing Wentworth's hand at parting and trying to infuse into his clasp all the sympathy he could not well utter, he found himself alone with Dr. Boulton in that gentleman's comfortable little brougham. Then some at least of his pent-up indignation broke forth.

"You might really have been more merciful to Wentworth, Boulton," he said. " Poor fellow, poor fellow! Whatever his past errors may have been, he is expiating them now in a way which may well make any man sorry for him. Faugh! these scandal-mongering journalists, who spend their time prying into the darkest corners of a man's life, if haply they may be able to unearth and drag to light some dead and buried shame of his past to blot his present with! Heaven may forgive and forget, but the society papers, never."

"Wentworth is an uncommonly good actor," retorted the other coolly. " That scene with the

child when he came in was the best thing I ever
saw him do yet.   It was, in its way, quite consummate.   Only don't mistake very perfect art
for nature, my dear sir."

"Did it ever occur to you that it was possible
to make the converse mistake ?" Sir George
asked.

"How ?"

"To mistake nature for art.   The man was
carried completely out of himself for the moment.
How else do you account for a proud man like
Wentworth voluntarily making such a statement
as he made to you and me subsequently ?   Poor
fellow !"

"He is a deucedly clever fellow, at any rate,"
murmured Dr. Boulton obstinately.   "He knows
how to pose, and how to turn his very humilia-
tions to account.   Supposing all this tale had
come out through the poor girl herself, would he
have shown up quite so well ?   Especially as she
is dying, to a certainty.   I had little hope of
saving her yesterday, and I have next to none
to-day.   Do you see any chance for her ?" he
asked, after a minute's pause, as his companion
preserved an impenetrable silence.

"No, humanly speaking, none.   She is dying,
undoubtedly."

CHAPTER VI.

"BY THE VISITATION OF GOD."

*"Behold, I take away from thee the desire of thine eyes with a stroke."—*Ezek. xxiv. 16.

Yes, she was dying. They all knew it: the doctors, the nurse, the faithful Dickinson, the very servants of the house. Margaret knew it, though she never spoke of it; Wentworth knew it, though he never acknowledged it even to himself. At last, when two more days and nights had gone wearily by, they saw that Stella herself knew it also, and accepted her fate with the quiet resignation which comes so often, even to the very young and happy, when really about to die. "I shall not get well now, Aunt Margaret," she said, when the third morning came, and she had struggled back to consciousness again for a while; and Margaret dared not contradict her. Wentworth, who was in the room, but standing

just out of sight, moved suddenly into view, and
then turned and went out without speaking.
Stella looked after him wistfully.

"I did not know he was there," she observed.
"Still, he must have known soon. Poor father!"
Her pity was all for Wentworth; regret for her-
self seemed scarcely to exist at all.

But it was not often that she could talk even
so much as this. A great part of her time was
spent in a kind of heavy stupor, which to Wentworth's uninitiated eye often looked so like sleep,
that he could hardly credit the doctors' assurances
that it had nothing in common with health-giving
slumber. At first this frequent unconsciousness
of Stella's seemed to her father the worst of trials,
but he soon learnt to prefer it to her waking
moments, when he had nothing to do but stand
by and contemplate the sufferings, physical and
mental, which he and all others were often
alike powerless to relieve. Throughout those
forty-eight hours, long because so full of pain,
yet short because he knew they must be the last
of Stella's ebbing life, Wentworth was writhing
under that worst of tortures—a torture which
almost every human being is destined at some
time or other to endure—the sense of utter
helplessness in the presence of a distress which

he would gladly have given his own life to alleviate.

Nor could he hide from himself the most cruel fact of all, that this distress, in so far as it was mental and not physical, was his own handiwork. With the return of her fever at night, Stella still wandered in mind from time to time, and though she spoke few coherent sentences, and her delirium was never of the painful or violent kind, yet she let fall enough for Wentworth to see that the shadow of that dark burden which had so long oppressed her mind still rested upon it. Her eager inquiry, " What did I say last night, Aunt Margaret ? " when complete self-recollection returned with morning light, was to him a daily-recurring martyrdom.

The third time she put it, he stepped forward and answered it himself. " Nothing of any consequence, my darling. Don't trouble yourself about what you say or don't say. It is no matter : for you have no secret to keep now, remember. I know all about it."

" It is for other people," she urged faintly.

"Other people know already," he answered with reckless frankness; "you could tell them nothing fresh. Other people don't think of your father quite as you do, sweet. For you

love me still, my child, don't you? Just as
before?"

"Why shouldn't I?" Stella asked, trying to
stroke his hair with very feeble, tremulous fingers.
"Nothing could make any difference—in that
way. Only—I was sorry. It seemed so dreadful to think that they could write so of—of
you."

She stopped a moment, with a new hope
breaking suddenly in upon her mind. What
if, after all, her suffering had been causeless?
What if the accusations of *Town Talk* had been
mere lying slanders, and Mrs. Arlingham a
false or over-credulous witness to their truth?
"Father," she asked, with the boldness and
directness that death, known to be close at hand,
gave her, "it wasn't true, was it—what they
said of you? I can't think now why I ever
believed it."

Wentworth's heart seemed to stand still for
an instant. Then he averted his face, and
answered almost harshly, "Some of it was false,
Stella—a good deal of it. But not all."

She made no rejoinder. Only, after a minute,
her weak arm clasped his neck more closely, and
she moved her head on the pillow so that her
cheek might rest against his hair.

"Well, darling," he said at last, "I had to tell you the bitter truth."

"I told you it made no difference—no difference at all," the girl replied in a stronger voice. "Except that I love you more, because I know you must be unhappy. I wish I could stay with you now."

"You will be better off—elsewhere," he returned, hardly knowing what he said.

"Yes," Stella assented simply, as if the assertion admitted of no question. "But you will want me, I know."

"Don't trouble yourself about my wants. I am not worth any sorrow, darling."

"I am only sorry because I thought you were quite perfect. But it does not matter. You will be, some time."

"Your faith in me is great, my child," he answered as soon as he could speak, unconsciously using the very same words he had used to another three days before. And after that they talked no more, then or at any time, for the flame of Estelle Wentworth's earthly existence had well-nigh died down in the socket, and this conversation was its last flicker of brightness before it finally went out for ever.

All through that day she was beset with pain

and restlessness, but as night came on—the third
night after Wentworth reached London, and the
sixth of her illness—she grew, contrary to her
usual custom, easier and more tranquil. The
doctors paid their usual evening visit about nine
o'clock, and gave Margaret her instructions for
the night, Dr. Boulton expressing his belief that
it would be a more comfortable one than his
patient had had yet. But Sir George Carmichael, when Wentworth looked to him for
confirmation of this favourable opinion, preserved an obstinate and discouraging silence,
only saying into Margaret's ear as he passed
out, "Keep a close watch upon her, and don't
hesitate to rouse her for the cordial, if necessary.
I see signs of a change."

About midnight Margaret sent the nurse away
to rest in the adjoining room, and herself took
the watch—a watch shared by Wentworth, who
had never once thought of sleep since the hour
of his arrival, except such sleep as he could
snatch at brief intervals in the daytime. It was
a very quiet watch, broken only by the administration of the cordial at regular intervals; for
on this night Stella neither moaned nor wandered
—she lay comparatively still.

About two o'clock in the morning there was a

slight attack of breathlessness and restlessness, lasting five minutes or so. Wentworth, who till then had been standing at the foot of his daughter's bed, now changed his position to a chair beside it, and Stella soon sank into her former half-conscious condition again, with her head partially supported on his shoulder. Margaret sat by the fire, and trimmed it noiselessly from time to time.

The hours went by, and none of the three occupants of the room seemed to stir. Stella's breathing grew gradually quieter and less painfully audible; Wentworth sat on like a figure of stone; Margaret looked from the father and child to the fire and back again. She knew well enough that it was only a question of hours now with Stella, and how would Paul bear his life in the future, she wondered? How, when the present tension was at an end, would he endure his recent discovery of the nature of Stella's haunting secret? For Margaret, too, had by this time learnt all the meaning of that pitiful mystery.

Still the hours went by. The sickly dawn was beginning to steal into the room, and Margaret softly put out the now useless night-lamp. The little clock opposite her on the mantelpiece

pointed to twenty-five minutes past five; in forty
minutes it would be time for Stella's cordial
again.

Ah! a falling coal awoke her from her involuntary slumber of exhaustion. She was on her
feet instantly, shivering as one only does in the
chill of dawn, and wild with terror lest she
should have overslept herself. No, thank God!
she had not been asleep more than half an hour.
The hands of the little timepiece stood only at
five minutes to six; but it was fully day now,
and as Margaret turned towards the bed, she
saw Wentworth rise to his feet and lay Stella
gently back on her pillows. He stood looking
at her a moment, took up her hands and kissed
them tenderly, one after another—"How foolish!"
thought Margaret, "and how likely to disturb
her!"—and then fell back in his former attitude,
with his arms crossed over his breast, gazing
down upon her.

Margaret poured out the cordial, and advanced
with it from the other side. So far Wentworth
had not seemed to observe his sister's movements, but now he made her a warning gesture,
so fierce almost in its mute vehemence, that she
started back. She stood irresolute a few seconds;
then, setting down the glass, she crept round to

her brother's side with an undefined terror at her heart, and laid her hand on his arm.   "Paul!" she said appealingly.

He did not reply.

"Paul!"—more urgently still.   "Is she asleep, do you think?"

Wentworth turned and faced her—faced her with a look which to her dying day Margaret will never forget, and which, for its fixed anguish of despair, she prays she may never again behold on the face of any human creature.   "No," he answered very quietly.   "She is dead—quite dead."

CHAPTER VII.

THE WORST OF IT.

"And your sentence is written all the same,
And I can do nothing—pray perhaps!"
R. BROWNING.

"IT came upon me as a shock at the last; I had no idea the end was really so very near at hand," Margaret said, brushing away a few quiet tears. "Of course Sir George had spoken of a change, and that expression of his alarmed me at first; but afterwards all the change I saw seemed to be a change for the better. Not that I cherished any actual hope of her recovery; but she seemed so much easier and quieter. Well, it was very merciful that it should have been so. There was nothing more we could have done. Only it seemed so terrible that I should have slept through those last few moments."

"I understand that," Muriel rejoined gently,

with a compassionate glance at Margaret, whose
mourning dress seemed to emphasize the extreme
pallor of her worn, delicate face. "Did your
brother expect it, do you think?"

The cloud of sorrowful recollection on Margaret's features deepened into a darker shade of
present anxiety. She shook her head slightly.
"I hardly know," she replied. "He never spoke
to me about her state before she died, further
than to put such questions as he desired to have
answered; and he always received my replies
without comment. All through those dreadful
three days I was telling you of, he never once
remarked to me that she seemed better or worse.
And since—oh! since I have not dared to speak
of her at all."

"Is that well?"

"No, it is not at all well," Margaret acknowledged. "But I dare not, Muriel, I dare not.
Though I am so fond of Paul, I believe I have
always been a little afraid of him; and to intermeddle with such grief as his is more than I can
adventure. Yet it is dreadful leaving him to
himself. If only Philip were here! He may be
by to-morrow, perhaps."

"How long is it since you sent for him?"

"I wrote more than a fortnight ago—just the

day after; but I could only direct the letter to the *poste restante* at Bergen, to wait for him there. He intended going to Iceland first, and returning by way of Norway to Sweden, when he started; but he had not made up his mind how long he should be on the road. It depended a good deal on how fast he picked up; he has overworked very much of late. I had such scruples about bringing him home any sooner, that I did not actually ask him to come; I only just stated facts, and left him to judge for himself."

"He will be sure to come," said Muriel, with conviction. "But in the mean time——"

"In the mean time, can I do nothing, you mean? Muriel, if you saw Paul as he is now, you would know that he is quite beyond anything I could possibly do for him. What can I say? Philip might help him, perhaps; no one else."

At ordinary times Margaret Irvine might and did often think of her younger brother as a visionary, a dreamer, an enthusiast, though she was far too loyal to stigmatize him openly by such names; but now, in this "strait and dreadful pass" in life, she turned to him with instinctive confidence as her one possible counsellor, his brother's one possible helper. Since he lived in habitual contemplation of the mysteries of life and death, he might just possibly have a word to say on this one.

"Did you write to Paul yourself at all?" Margaret asked presently, breaking the silence that had succeeded her last speech. "He had a great many kind letters of sympathy, I believe, though he never showed any of them to me."

"No; oh no!"—with an irrepressible shudder. "How could *I* possibly write to *him?*" Then, catching a startled look on Margaret's face, Muriel recovered herself by an effort, and explained, "Letters from outsiders at such a time are little better than a mockery. Would it have helped your brother in the least to know that one person more was sorry for him?"

"I don't know," said Margaret. "I thought you might have said something helpful, perhaps; you have such a helpful way with you sometimes. And then"—with a faint flush overspreading her face—"you knew what no one else did, you see."

Muriel pressed her hands together on her knee. "Don't remind me of that, for pity's sake," she said. "Though why should I ask you not to speak of it, when I can think of nothing else?

It was my fault, my fault! Margaret, you must
be mad to talk of my writing to your brother
in his grief—I, who am the very cause of it!
He may well feel that, but for me, his child
might be alive now. Yet I meant so well, so
well—for him and her both. God knows I
did!"

Margaret rose from her chair, and slid on to
her knees beside Muriel. "My dear child," she
said, pressing Muriel's cold fingers in her own,
"who doubts you—who blames you? Not Paul,
I am sure. He knows you acted for his good,
his happiness——"

"Yes," Muriel interrupted; "just so. It was
for his good, his happiness, I acted; I forgot her.
I deceived myself—wilfully, I begin to think
now. I put her aside, and persuaded myself
that in sparing him I was sparing her also, when
in reality I was not considering her at all. I
judged her by myself. What right had I to do
so? Because I, a woman accustomed to play a
part and keep every feeling that would shame
me in the eyes of the world a profound secret,
until I have become a mere hollow mask to
myself as well as to every one else, could have
borne the burden I laid on that innocent child,
was that a reason for concluding she could bear

it also ? The silent falsehood which would have been nothing to me killed her !"

"Hush, hush !" Margaret said soothingly. "Don't accuse yourself so wildly. If you erred, it was an error of judgment which the wisest, as well as the kindest, might have committed. And the real cause of this terrible trouble lies other-where than with you, as Paul knows too well. It is that which has shattered him so utterly. It is not his grief which is driving him to despair; it is his remorse. I might have com-forted him as regards his sorrow ; as regards the rest I am powerless. That is why I say to myself a hundred times a day, 'If Philip were only here !'"

"Supposing he were," Muriel answered, "what do you think he would say ? "

"I think he would say," said Margaret slowly, "that it was perhaps well that this had hap-pened; more, that it was undoubtedly well. From Philip's point of view I don't see that he could say anything else. Even from mine—which is not altogether his—I can see that it may be so."

She rose hurriedly from her kneeling position, and began nervously to mend the small fire which was smouldering in the grate. "I have never spoken about the one shadow on the brilliancy of Paul's life and career to any human being before," she said rapidly; "but—-well, you know now. I suppose you knew before, after a fashion; most people do. He was never hypocritical; if anything, he made rather the worst of himself than otherwise, dear fellow! For he is so dear, so capable of good, so full of fine impulses towards better things, Muriel. I am his sister, and I know. I don't speak of his talents—no one can say that his intellectual gifts have not been well employed; I speak of what he might be, and what—even in spite of all his falls and faults—he is, in himself."

"I understand; I believe you."

"Then," Margaret said, turning round suddenly, "don't you see—for I am beginning to see—that if one believes, as you and I do, in 'a Power not ourselves that makes for righteousness,' one may well expect that it would not allow a life which might have been so noble to be hopelessly marred, while yet there remained any means of restoring it to its original self? And supposing this were the only way?"

"It is a very strange way."

"Philip, if he were here, would tell you that it is by strange ways the world is governed," said Margaret, with a faint smile. Then she left the fire and went back to her seat again.

"Muriel," she said, after a minute or two, as her friend showed no disposition to break silence, "I don't want you to judge Paul too harshly. He has had his extenuating circumstances; I don't say that they excuse, much less that they justify him, but they do at least explain him. He was always, unfortunately, impulsive and sensitive and impressionable, but I verily believe all might have gone well with him notwithstanding, if his nature had not been warped by his circumstances. It would have been so easy to have led him right through his affections! As it was, his unhappy marriage simply threw him back upon himself, and all that abnormal craving for sympathy which has been his lifelong bane was left worse than unsatisfied. Poor Alice! I do not want to speak harshly of her in her grave, but I find it hard to forgive her even now. He worshipped her so intensely, Muriel; if it had not been for incurable frivolity and invincible hardness, she could never have lost him. But I do not think she cared to keep him; he was too much trouble. His very affection was a nuisance to her, poor shallow soul!

"I think Paul has never got over the shock of

that first blow—I mean, the discovery that Alice never cared for him in reality," Margaret continued presently. "I suppose it shook his trust in womanhood altogether. At least—for I think she had before her death effectually killed all love for herself in him—-that is how I interpret his showing no inclination to marry again, which I half hoped he might have done."

"You hoped that ?"

"I half hoped it—if Paul could have fallen in love with a really noble, womanly woman, and she had loved him in return, it might have been like the opening of a new life to him. But I did not dare hope it altogether."

"Why not ?" Muriel asked.

"Because I could hardly hope that the kind of woman I should have desired for his wife, the woman who might be his salvation, as I imagine, would ever consent to marry him ? Do you think she would ? "

"If she loved him," Muriel responded half audibly.

"Even if she loved him, and therefore consented to overlook his past, she might still be afraid—afraid to trust his future—so it always seemed to me. Now such a dream seems further off than ever."

" Because this loss has swallowed up every other feeling ? "

" No, because it has unfitted him to make any woman happy. With this cloud of perpetual remorse upon him, what could he do except bring the shadow of it upon any one who loved him supremely ? And nothing short of supreme love could be any help to him."

" And what do you suppose the shadow would count for, with such love as you speak of ? " Muriel demanded, with a sharp ring of scorn in her voice. " For nothing, for less than nothing— except to increase and deepen the love a hundred-fold."

" If love like that were to be found at all," Margaret replied sadly. " It is at least too rare for us to hope to find it within the compass of our own lives. Besides, what right has Paul to expect an affection wholly unselfish, wholly self-forgetting, looking for no happiness beyond that of lightening by a little the weight of his suffering, self-wrought as it chiefly is ? I do not ask so much for him, nor he for himself. A woman, be she ever so devoted, has a right to look for some happiness where she gives her love."

" Do you think," Muriel asked, with a strange

fixed look, "that love and happiness ever go together ? "

"My dear Muriel!" Margaret exclaimed. "Yes, surely I think so. I know it, indeed," she added, a tremulous smile just wavering on her lips. She had been very happy herself once in days of which she never spoke now, but of which the fragrant recollection often made her happy yet.

"Your experience has been different from mine, then," Muriel retorted bitterly. "Do you call it happiness to be dependent on another person's most careless word, or capricious look, or passing inflection of voice for your very life ? To be such a slave to some man—in whose estimation you rank very likely as a mere plaything, an object of the most trifling amusement —that a sharp sentence from him, or a cold 'good morning,' makes the whole world dark to you; so that your existence is one long dread of displeasing him, even when he is most tender and kind ? Is it happiness to know that he is everything to you; that health, position, money, every friend and relation you have, are nothing as set against an hour in his presence; and that to him you are a faint interest, a means of gratifying his vanity, at best an agreeable companion, a woman he has 'a fancy for,' such as he has had and will have again for a score of others ? Do you call this happiness—this long misery of hope and fear, when you imagine yourself loved in the morning, and find yourself forgotten before the day is out ?"

"No, no!" Margaret rejoined hastily. "But you generalize too much, Muriel. Where there is real confidence, real mutual trust——"

"Trust!" Muriel broke in. "Did I say there was no trust—that there was not trust the most absolute, the most unsuspecting, confidence amounting to idolatry, both in the man and in his love ? What then ? Yes, what then ? When the day comes on which you find out that all this was based on a falsehood, on a hideous fraud, the discovery of which has killed everything— reverence, belief, honour—everything except the love which makes your life an agony ;—will you tell me to be happy then ?"

Margaret was struck dumb with astonishment. Was this impassioned creature the self-contained woman she had known so intimately for years past ? That Muriel was an unhappy wife she had divined long ago ; but what was there in Geoffrey Arlingham to have stirred at any time such depths of passionate feeling as Muriel revealed ?

"The love ought to die too," Muriel went on, heedless of Margaret's silence; "but supposing it will not? Supposing it cannot? Is it happiness to live in a perpetual struggle with it? Is it happiness to be separated from what you love in such a way and by such a barrier that, though it is torture to be apart, it is far worse torture to meet? Is it happiness to know that when he is triumphant, you must not feel glad? Or to see him suffering, suffering intolerably, and not dare say a word of comfort, however much you suffer with him? Worst of all, to see the evil growing stronger and the good weaker in him as the years go by, and still to be able to do nothing—yet you know there is no escape for you. Though not only all the sorrows, but all the sins, seem to fall on you and crush you down as if they were your own, you can do nothing—only go on loving, loving to your own unspeakable wretchedness!"

She broke off suddenly and walked across to the window, where she stood looking out into the street.

"And then to remember," she added half audibly, "that but for your own wicked folly it might have all been yours to do."

Again Margaret did not speak. A kind of

helpless terror took possession of her; she felt
desperately afraid, and dared not ask herself of
what. So great was this terror that all compassion for Muriel remained for the moment in
abeyance. It only awoke tardily when, after
some minutes, her friend came back to her side,
and laid a timid hand on her shoulder.

"Margaret," she said quite quietly—she was
a little pale and tremulous, but otherwise perfectly herself again—"I surprised you very much
just now, I am certain. You did not understand
what I meant, did you?"

"No, dear, no," Margaret faltered. She would
not have understood for worlds.

"I have held the opinions I enunciated this
evening for many years," Muriel went on, with a
miserable attempt at a smile; "and I had just
a little temporary fit of mania, which made me
give utterance to them for once. I am sorry to
have shocked you, but it has done me good to
speak, and you need think no more about it;
neither need I, since happily you did not understand. Promise me that you will never try to
understand, Margaret."

And Margaret promised.

CHAPTER VIII.

IN THE VALLEY OF ACHOR.

"And seven days he walked through it, by a path which few can tell; for those that have trodden it like least to speak of it, and those who go there again in dreams are glad enough when they awake."—C. KINGSLEY.

"I WILL try to arrange what you wish about the concert, Philip. I must see one or two people, and secure their help, before I go into the final arrangements with you, but by the day after to-morrow I dare say we may be able to put the affair on a practical footing."

"Very well; I will look in again on Friday, then. And now I suppose I had better be off, for the rain has stopped, and I have no end of things to do before dark."

"Put on your coat before you go down," Margaret responded, moving to fetch the garment in question from the back drawing-room. "We may call this summer, but to me it feels positively wintry. How is your cough, Phil ? Really better ? "

" Really gone," Irvine replied, accepting the coat with an indulgent smile. "It is quite a thing of the past now. My holiday in the north effected wonders."

" I was afraid it had been cut too short to be of any use at all," Margaret said. "How did you think Paul looking when you saw him last ? " she asked abruptly, twisting one of Irvine's buttons round and round in her fingers.

" Very worn and ill indeed. Of course he said he was all right, and evidently resented my making any remark on his personal appearance whatever. The affectation of cheerfulness he tries to keep up with me is pitiably transparent, and infinitely sadder to witness than any out-ward show of grief could be."

Tears were in Margaret's eyes. " Mr. Orme met him coming out of the House on Thursday —it was the night of the division on the Welsh Riots Bill, and he had been down to vote—and told Lady Beatrice afterwards that he thought Paul's smile now was the saddest thing he ever saw. Has he never said anything at all to you, Philip ? "

" Not a word since his utter breakdown when

we first met a month ago. That was complete
enough while it lasted, and appalling to witness
—I am thankful you were spared it—but even
then he hardly said anything, and he has been
entirely reserved since. Only once, when he
was in a very bitter mood, he remarked that
he thought I had hardly magnified my office in
the matter of preaching and exhortation as he
should have expected."

" And you—what did you say ? "

" I told him I thought the preaching had been
done so forcibly, without the intervention of any
human instrument, that there was nothing left
for me to say. He only answered, 'Anyhow, I
thank you for your consideration in sparing me
useless homilies,' and then went on to speak of
something else. That was three weeks ago
now."

" I had hoped so much that he would turn to
you, and that you would be able to help him,"
Margaret murmured despondently.

" I don't think this is a case for any one's
help. 'Every man must bear his own burden.' "

Margaret flushed nervously. " Don't be angry
with me, Philip, but—are you quite sure that
you went just the right way to work ? He
must want comfort so much."

"There I disagree with you entirely," Irvine answered with a sudden accession of sternness. " His is not a wound to be soothed and salved ; it is a just suffering to be endured."

"You are hard, Philip ; I think you are unmercifully hard. Surely Paul's grief is terrible enough to make one forget all about his past errors."

" Call them by their right name—sins," said Irvine, more sternly still. " There is nothing gained and a great deal sacrificed by giving soft names to ugly realities. But I should be very sorry, Margaret, if I thought this was a case of mere grief, or even of mere remorse. I think— I hope I am not mistaken—that it is something quite different."

" What ?" Margaret asked.

" Self-revelation. Therefore it is a process with which I have neither the right nor the wish to intermeddle. It is in all men's lives a terribly painful process ; in Paul's case I can well believe that it must needs be a torture surpassing words. But if I could, I would not try to soften it."

Margaret repeated, " I think you are cruelly hard."

" Then you think the Divine laws hard too,"

Irvine rejoined quietly. " But it is the old story of which we were speaking just now. Because Paul is dear to you, therefore his suffering is above all other suffering: you are full of pity for him, but indifferent to all else. Even in what we know—in his present trouble, for instance—see what misery he brought on others ! And what of the rest ? If the sum of all his reckless self-indulgence has wrought were reckoned together, do you think we could venture to say that his punishment, great as it is—God perhaps only knows how great—is too great to be just ? "

Margaret was appalled into silence. Why was it that, as her brother spoke the solemn and terrible words which closed her lips to further argument, there came ringing back on her ears words uttered a few weeks earlier, in the same place, by a woman's voice ? " *What then ? When the day comes on which you find that all this was based on a falsehood, on a hideous fraud, the discovery of which has killed everything in you —reverence, belief, honour—everything except the love which makes your life an agony ;—will you tell me to be happy then ?* " What had Muriel and her secret heart-wound to do with the matter ?

" You see, it was the same with Paul himself."

Irvine went on, seeing his sister made no rejoinder. " Evil never showed itself to him fully
as evil, till it touched the thing he loved. Then,
indeed—— It is always like that, more or
less."

" I wonder what induced him to send for
Mabel so suddenly ? " Margaret said musingly.
" He was quite determinedly set against her
returning home when I ventured to advise it
just before you came back, and said that if
it was not convenient to me to keep her, he
should send her to the Chamberlains. You
did not persuade him to alter his decision, I
suppose ? "

" I said nothing to him ; I saw it would be
useless. But I told Mabel she had better write
and ask permission herself to come home, which
I believe she did at once; and you saw the
result. You will probably have her back again
before long, though, I am afraid, if Paul goes to
America."

" Do you think he really will go ? "

" He had pretty well made up his mind to it
on Sunday. Perhaps it might be the best thing
for him just now—that is, if he took Mabel with
him. But I fear he is determined to go alone.
However, I am going to dine with him to-

morrow night, and then I shall hear what his final decision on the whole question is. I can tell you about it on Friday. Good-bye till then."

But when the time for dining with his brother arrived, it did not seem likely that Irvine would have much to communicate to his sister on the morrow. Wentworth kept up the conversation during the *tête-à-tête* dinner with unflagging persistency, but never allowed it to wander for a moment from general subjects; and the presence of the servants, indeed, forbade any strictly personal discussion. With the hour of dessert Mabel appeared, looking dignified and almost womanly in her crape evening dress and jet ornaments, and thenceforward her father's attention was wholly given to her. So unwilling was he to part from her for a moment, that he proposed their all adjourning to the drawing-room together, since Irvine took no wine. And Irvine could not well oppose the proposition, though he was profoundly disappointed at losing the opportunity of exchanging a few words with his brother in private.

The opportunity occurred after all, however. Mabel was summoned to give audience to a dressmaker, who, for some occult reason best

known to herself, had chosen this very unseason-
able hour in the evening for the ceremony
known as "fitting on" various garments, and
had to leave her father and uncle. "Don't be
long, darling," the former said wistfully as she
rose to go. "Remember, I shall be on my way
to America in a few days; let me see as much
as I can of you now."

"She will take some little time, I know," was
Mabel's response. "I don't think it will be
worth while my coming down again to-night."

"Oh yes, it will!" Wentworth rejoined, with
an eagerness positively painful. "Come down
for a little while, Mab. I will give you half
an hour's 'extension of time,' if you come back
quickly."

As soon as the door had closed behind the
young girl, Wentworth threw himself back in
his chair and began talking rapidly, as if bent,
at all costs, on preventing Irvine's choosing his
own topics of conversation.

"Where are you ensconced now?" he asked,
while Irvine was noting with concern the deep
hollows which the last few weeks had made in
his temples, the darkness under his sunken eyes,
which betrayed a sleeplessness not of one but
many nights' duration, and the feverish bright-

ness of the eyes themselves. "Are you back at your old quarters?"

"No, I am still in Holly Street. It is an out-lying part of St. Lucy-at-Ford, away from the river; the water-side missions don't touch it, and even the City missionaries seem hardly to have found it out. It is rather a difficult place to get at."

"You will go back to Bethnal Green eventu-ally, I suppose?"

"I think not. I believe I shall stay where I am."

"Why do you make the change? Are the St. Lucy-at-Fordites specially encouraging specimens of ruffianism?"

"So far, quite the reverse. But one cannot expect to accomplish very much single-handed."

"These single-handed contests—one to ten thousand—sound very fine on paper and in platform speeches," Wentworth remarked, "but in practice I doubt their success. Why don't you stay at Bethnal Green, where at any rate there is a regular organization, and therefore a better chance of making some permanent im-pression on the great mass of brutality? I say nothing against your sacrificing yourself to these ideas, if such is your pleasure; but I protest against your throwing away strength and talents on a purely quixotic enterprise. It is such a waste of material, such a pouring of treasure into the well of the Danaides."

"Even so it would not be altogether wasted, from a Christian point of view," Irvine said. "However, I quite agree with you as to putting every talent to a tangible use, and there is really nothing quixotic about this affair. The Bethnal Green parish I worked in formerly being now, as you say, fully organized, can very well dispense with me; and the Holly Street district, on the other hand, has literally no one at present, for the Rector of St. Lucy's and his two curates are overwhelmed with the care of the water-side population alone, and the Nonconforming bodies have overlooked it strangely. So I concluded it my duty to move there, and endeavour to break up a little fresh ground."

"You seem to like the roughest places you can find," said Wentworth. "It is hard work to be always pioneering."

"Somebody must make the first breach in the wall," Irvine answered in a matter-of-fact way. "If you have been trained to that special part of the work, and have chosen to join yourself to that particular corps in the army, it is simply your business to go and make it. I am glad to say, though, that I shall not long be single-handed in Holly Street. Young Lister is coming to join me there after the middle of the Long Vacation."

" What Lister ?   Not the son of the Conservative M.P. for Chadgrove ? "

" One of his sons.   He has four, I believe; this is the third."

" You will fall out in your politics before the October term comes round," said Wentworth, with a mechanical attempt at a smile such as that which had struck Mr. Orme with compassion in the lobby of the House of Commons.   " No scion of the house of Lister will ever be able to swallow your transcendental Radicalism.   I cannot imagine how Lister *père* can contemplate without horror the notion of one of his darling boys being exposed to the influence of such contaminating ideas."

" We serve a common Master," said Irvine quietly.   " The rest is more or less a matter of detail.   By the way, I am the bearer of a sort of message to you from Lister himself.   He mentioned, when I saw him yesterday, that he had heard incidentally you were going to America, and wanted to know if you had found a pair as yet—if not, he would be glad to pair with you

for the remainder of the session. He is going on
a sea-voyage himself, for the benefit of his throat.
I told him I knew nothing of your arrangements,
of course, but I would mention the subject to
you, and you would write to him about it."

"I am infinitely obliged to him, but my
arrangements are made already, as it happens."
Wentworth spoke curtly, as if he did not care to
be further communicative.

The curiosity of Irvine, usually the least curious
of men, was fairly roused.

"Who is your pair?" he asked. "I fancied
you might have had difficulty in finding one
just now."

"Very likely," was the reply. "But I have
not been in search of a pair. I wrote this
afternoon to apply for the Chiltern Hundreds."
Wentworth was evidently taking enormous pains
to speak with perfect indifference, as if the fact
he announced was one of no possible interest or
importance to himself or any one else. "I don't
know when it may be convenient for me to
return from America; perhaps I shall try my
hand at founding a new state there—if I can
find a piece of unoccupied ground for the experiment," he added, with a half-laugh.

Irvine rose involuntarily from his chair with

an exclamation of dismay. "You have actually resigned your seat?"

"Well!" returned Wentworth impatiently, with a defiant look directed full at his brother. "What then? I know what you want to say: waste of talents and opportunities, duty to the country, etc., etc. Cannot the sermon be taken as preached? By all means deliver it if you like, though; but I warn you that I know all the arguments already, and could answer them beforehand, if I chose."

Irvine's lips compressed themselves closely for a moment before he answered, "You are mistaken. I have no sermon to deliver. I have one question to ask, and one only. Do not you think that self-revenge would be a nobler course for the future than an unavailing attempt to revenge one's self on God?"

Wentworth grew very pale, but his look did not waver. "You bring strange accusations, and use strong language, Philip Irvine," was all his reply.

"I acknowledge it. But I am accustomed to speak the truth plainly, as you know. This act of yours is an act of revenge, and assuredly not of self-revenge, except in so far as it partakes of the nature of a soul-suicide. I leave you to decide against whom the vengeance is directed."

"You draw reckless and rather unwarrantable conclusions from such a simple proceeding as the resignation of a seat in Parliament," said Wentworth, with white lips. .

"Because the act is only the final link in a chain of such acts; because—pardon me, Paul, but I cannot speak less than the unvarnished truth—it is the logical result of a life lived on the principle of indemnifying self at the cost of rebellion and lawlessness for that which is not lawfully given. It was the very principle acted on the other day by those poor fellows whose cause you branded me as a Socialist for espousing in a measure, when the punishment legally their due fell upon them. What, I ask you, had been given *them?* A childhood spent in ignorance and degradation, followed by a manhood of exhausting and repulsive labour, sordid want, and perpetual disappointment, with everything to tempt them to vice and everything to repel them from virtue. So they indemnified themselves by attacking God and society—the one with their voices, and the other with their bludgeons—and you condemned them as miscreants. You had, as far as man can see, every

earthly blessing a man can desire, except—forgive
my reference—one, possibly—— "

"Except the one which would have made the
rest worth having; except the one the absence
of which rendered all the rest valueless," interrupted Wentworth. "Philip, I have listened to
you more patiently than most men would have
done under the circumstances; but you are a
strange fellow, and it is difficult to quarrel with
you. Only, for Heaven's sake, don't talk of what
you don't understand—you who never loved a
woman, and therefore cannot possibly guess what
an utter wreck her faithlessness may make of a
man's life."

"There," said Irvine, with a quiver of the lip,
after a brief struggle with himself, "you err.
You err greatly. It has been my desire to place
my hopes above and beyond this world, and I
believe I am upheld in this endeavour; if I were
not, my life would be past endurance. And I
have been more lightly dealt with, I admit—
there was no question of anything but the purest
faith in the woman I loved and shall always
love—but if you imagine I know nothing of the
bitterness of a lonely life and an unsatisfied
longing, yes, and of the sharpness of self-reproach too, you have judged hastily."

Irvine spoke with rising agitation. He had stripped off the veil which shrouded his dearest secret in answer to his brother's outbreak of pain and reproach, just as unhesitatingly as he would have performed any other painful act which he conceived to be a duty; but the sacrifice of his reserve had been a great one. Perhaps no one but Wentworth himself could have understood how great.

He laid his hand kindly for a moment on the younger man's shoulder. "I beg your pardon, Phil," he said huskily. "I am sorry to hear this. I hoped your life was altogether your own choice and pleasure."

"It *was* so," said Irvine, with a curious brightness in his eyes. "And it was too easy so, I suppose."

"Can nothing be done in the future?" Wentworth adventured. His quick sympathies were all aroused, and for the moment he had forgotten himself entirely.

"Nothing. My own deliberate choice has barred the way. It is all done with, for this world."

"She is—she is living, is she not?"

"I believe so," Irvine answered. The three words held all the fulness of his renunciation.

Wentworth took two or three turns up and down the room. "Well," he said at last, coming back, "you have not attempted any indemnification of self for what you lost, most assuredly. I certainly did; and how I have succeeded—how well I have succeeded," he repeated in a tone of such intense yet subdued anguish that Irvine, strong and steadfast as he was, felt himself fairly unmanned, "there is no need for me to tell you."

"Then, in God's name," said Irvine very solemnly, when he could speak again, "don't repeat the sin, and invite a repetition of the punishment. You have the child that is left you"—Wentworth started as if Irvine had stabbed him—"keep her with you, both for your sake and hers. And you have great powers and gifts, and a career before you which, so long as its rewards were of value in your eyes, you spared no pains to make for yourself. Why are you going to fling it all aside to idle away your intellectual prime of manhood in America?"

Wentworth slightly averted his head. "Because," he replied, "I may be better able to forget there what I cannot bear to remember."

"But you have no right to forget," said Philip Irvine.

Then Mabel came in again, and nothing more could be said that evening; and at the end of two days Irvine had not seen his brother again. But on the following Sunday afternoon Margaret came to pay him a visit in Holly Street, and while she was there, a note in Wentworth's handwriting was brought to him. He opened it; read it through slowly, twice; and then silently handed it to his sister across the table. It consisted only of a few lines.

"June 28th.

"DEAR PHILIP,

"I sail for New York from Liverpool to-morrow afternoon, taking Mabel and her governess with me. My love to Margaret. Say I will write or telegraph to her on landing.

"Your affectionate brother,

"PAUL WENTWORTH.

"P.S.—I have paired with Lister for the remainder of the session. Ellesthorpe and Orme are anxious that I should retain my seat, at any rate for the present, as they anticipate a general election in December or January."

CHAPTER IX.

"THE COLN INCIDENT."

"Shall I speak humbly now, who once was proud?"
E. B. BROWNING.

THE prognostications of Lord Ellesthorpe and
Mr. Orme proved to be perfectly correct. Soon
after the Houses rose in August, riots of a very
serious character broke out in Wales, necessi-
tating the passing of a Riots Bill far more
stringent in character than that which had become law during the previous June; and Parliament reassembled for a brief autumn session in
order to give effect to this measure, Ministers
undertaking, if provided with temporary powers
sufficiently large for the preservation of law and
order in the Principality, to appeal at once to the
country on the justice of the main point at issue
between the Government and those who were
beginning to be called "the rebels." The Bill

was passed, therefore; members returned to spend a rather anxious and unquiet Christmas in their more or less distant homes, and the writs went out for a general election in January.

There was the usual excitement and the usual turmoil — perhaps even more than the usual amount of wilful misrepresentation, reckless speech, and embittered writing. It was a contest in which men's minds became strung to a peculiarly high state of tension, and in which no quarter was given or taken on either side. Consequently, the number of venomous personal attacks made alike by party politicians and party journals waxed unusually large, and their character was marked by abnormal savageness of tone. The struggle was destined to become a veritable landmark in the private history of many of the combatants, by reason of the irreparable divisions it created between those who formerly met as friends outside the debatable ground of politics, and the breaches which it widened into impassable gulfs in the case of others who were in any sense of the word enemies.

Sir John Clavering, returning at the end of January from a year's cruise round the world, came to the conclusion that England was a much less desirable place than he had been wont to imagine when his yacht was floundering in the Atlantic rollers, or he himself was getting slowly fried by a tropical sun while lying-to, waiting for a breeze, in the South Pacific seas. Politically and socially, his native land appeared to him to have run mad on the Welsh scare; and climatically—well, with the streets of London rendered positively dangerous by an accumulation of half-melted snow which it seemed to be nobody's—perhaps because it was everybody's —business to clear away, and the atmosphere so murky that it was impossible for him to read his *Times* at midday without the help of candles, even such a sturdy old Briton as worthy Sir John might be pardoned for thinking regretfully of the even temperature of San Francisco, and wishing that he had deferred his return to his mother country until a more genial season of the year.

His patriotism and his temper were subjected on his first arrival to two additional trials, neither of which they could well support, but which, when combined, became altogether insupportable : a touch of rheumatism, and the absence of Lady Clavering, who had gone down to Brighton, like a dutiful daughter, to visit her parental home and her venerable parents after so long a separation as the late adventurous journey had entailed. Of course Sir John might have gone to Brighton too, had he chosen; but he did not choose. He had a rooted prejudice against Brighton after Christmas, just as he had a prejudice against using the steaming power of his yacht if it could possibly be avoided. But for his obstinate love of sailing, the *Mireille* need not have been so often lying-to in enforced inaction during his protracted voyage.

Sir John therefore stayed in London, abused the weather, grunted more than ever, and consoled himself as best he could by nursing his rheumatism, frequenting the Carlton, and dining with the few friends who were not still engaged in the political campaign. One of these was a certain Colonel Townsend, an elderly bachelor of large fortune, who had been greatly addicted to sport in general and the turf in particular during his earlier years, but who had long ago renounced all these pursuits, and his profession as well, in favour of literature at home and travel abroad. Sir John had managed to pick up a good deal of out-of-the-way information in the course of his wanderings, and this proved interesting to his friend, whose sense of humour was at the same time gratified by the highly original manner in which the said information was served up to the curious.

The two were dining together at Townsend's house one night, as frequently happened, when it suddenly occurred to Sir John Clavering to make an inquiry about his old young friends the Arlinghams. "By the way, Townsend," he said, "you know something of Arlingham, my Holmshire neighbour, don't you? Can you tell me if he and his wife happen to be in town just now? Lady Clavering would never forgive me if I omitted to look them up."

"They are certainly not in town, to the best of my belief," the other man replied. "I believe they are abroad. I know they left England directly after the final crash last October."

"Crash!" quoth Sir John gruffly. "What crash?"

"Do you mean to say you don't know that Arlingham has ruined himself—irretrievably, I'm afraid—on the turf?"

"How should I hear anything about it on the high seas?" demanded Sir John testily. "I was half-way to New Zealand in October last. Bless my soul! I'm excessively sorry. How did he contrive to do it?"

"The old story. A weak young fellow with more money than brains, and utterly unaccustomed to the management of wealth, falling into the hands of the Philistines in the shape of an unscrupulous crew who set him gambling on the turf and elsewhere—one knows the upshot of the story beforehand. I rather pity Arlingham—I believe folly and weakness are his chief crimes—and I am heartily sorry for his wife. Poor little soul! it must have been a rough awakening for her, if, as is supposed by most people, she had no previous inkling of the real state of affairs."

"Was the crash generally known to be impending?"

"Yes, very generally. Every one knew that Arlingham was heavily embarrassed before he went to Italy last winter, and it was said that he tried on that occasion to retrieve his fortunes by a course of heavy play at Monte Carlo—with the usual beneficial results. Then he came back, increased his racing stable, and lost a huge sum on the Derby—ran a horse at Longchamps for the Grand Prix whose performances caused even the Parisian *flâneur* to mock—finally made despairing efforts to recover himself at the autumn meetings, failed in everything, and had to confess himself utterly routed. After that he went off to the Continent again, having managed to turn his moor and the house at Rutland Gate into ready money. It is to be hoped he won't leave all that at Monte Carlo too."

Sir John sat aghast at his friend's story. "And Eversleigh?" he faltered. "Fortunately, though, that can't go to the hammer too."

"No, it is very strictly entailed. Eversleigh is let for a year only, I believe; but I should say it was highly improbable that Arlingham would be able to return and live there when the year is out. It is a deplorable affair altogether. Such a fine fortune almost entirely dissipated in three years!"

"It ought never to have been in Arlingham's power to dissipate it," Sir John answered indignantly.

"The old fellow in Australia died intestate, didn't he? I thought so. Well, it has always been my opinion that for a young man to have a big amount of capital at his absolute command in hard cash—as it seems Arlingham had—is about as unmixed a curse to him as may be, in the majority of cases."

"Do you know where they are—Arlingham and his wife?" Sir John asked, not without feeling. "I have known her all her life very nearly, poor child."

"I have no idea whatever, beyond the mere fact that they are out of England. There was quite an excitement about the affair at the time—Mrs. Arlingham was always popular, you know, and a good deal admired—but by this time it is all ancient history, and people have ceased to feel any interest in the matter. There have been other intermediate excitements, and now the election has for the moment absorbed everybody's thoughts.'

"Talking of the election," said Sir John, who for all his rough exterior had a warm heart, and was too genuinely moved by Muriel Arlingham's misfortunes to care to discuss them further with a man who felt only the interest of a passing acquaintance concerning her, "I am as much in the dark touching its ins and outs as I am with regard to the social events that have taken place lately. I want you to enlighten me on one or two points. First of all, what is meant by a mysterious allusion I have come upon more than once in the newspapers to some episode connected with the election at Coln ? It is generally referred to in a darkly oracular manner as 'The Coln Incident.'"

"Curious!" ejaculated Colonel Townsend. "Curious, I mean, that you should have come for information on that subject to me rather than to any one else, for I was present when the 'incident,' as the penny-a-liners are pleased to call it, took place."

"Indeed! I thought you eschewed politics and political campaigning altogether."

"So I do, as a rule. Party politics interest me very little. But this Welsh business is a national question," said the old soldier, drawing up his tall figure, " and every trueborn Englishman is bound to support the National party on such an occasion. In so far as I am a party man at all—which, as you know, is a very short way indeed—I suppose I may call myself a Conservative, but all those minor distinctions are obliterated just now. I knew Wentworth would have a hard fight to hold the seat for law-abiding Liberalism as against scarcely veiled Socialism, and, as I had some little property in the neighbourhood of Coln, I felt it my duty to go down and support him."

" H'm !" answered Sir John rather grudgingly. " Well, you may have been right—you may have been right."

"The constituency, which in the old days

before the last Franchise Bill used to be very
'blue' indeed, has grown extremely Radical of
late. When Wentworth won the seat two years
ago, it was by a very small majority over a
staunch Tory candidate. Now no Tory would
have the ghost of a chance in Coln. It was a
very moot point indeed this time whether the
weavers—weavers seem to have a constitutional
inclination for Socialism—would put up with
Wentworth's wide, majestic, Imperial-Liberal
views, if I may call them so, when contrasted
with the narrow rant and cant of the working-
man demagogue who opposed him. However,
things went better than I expected. Wentworth,
who came back from America only just in time
for the campaign, spoke magnificently on almost
every occasion, and his meetings grew fuller and
more enthusiastic every night."

"He is always a fine speaker," said Sir John.

"He was never finer than at Coln last month.
Well, you may imagine that this did not suit the
other side's game at all. They were at their
wits' end. So, as Clay could not succeed in
talking Wentworth down, he began to write him
down; and being a coarse fellow without much
regard for truth and none for good feeling, you
may fancy that he did not stick at trifles to

gain his end. There is a vile little newspaper published in Coln which is devoted to Clay's interests—a kind of *Eatanswill Gazette,* you understand—and this pestilential print began to fill its columns day after day with covert insinuations against Wentworth's character."

Colonel Townsend paused to stir the fire, and then resumed again: "Wentworth, as we all know, though a man of most brilliant parts and —I believe—of very noble disposition, has not altogether a flawless record to show as regards his earlier years. I don't suppose many of us have that; but he was always a reckless fellow, and so his indiscretions became more widely known than most men's. Of course this was a splendid card in the hands of the Socialists, and, if they had played it well, might have ruined us and him. Luckily they went a little too far. They got tired of hints and innuendoes, and proceeded to open slander. Do you remember a scandalous story about Wentworth which *Town Talk* ventured to publish a year ago, and which was afterwards withdrawn as false?"

Sir John nodded assent. "I remember. It was a good deal canvassed in the clubs at the time, but was proved in the end to be a pure invention."

"Exactly. Well, this story was reproduced in full by the *Coln Banner of Right*. Of course it made a profound impression, though Clay took care to keep his organ clear of an action for libel by having the withdrawal printed with it. I don't know, by the way, if you recollect that the withdrawal was made in such a form as to be almost more damaging than the original accusation?"

"No, I don't remember anything about it."

"Well, that I can show you; I kept filed copies of that admirable journal, the *Banner*, during the canvass." Colonel Townsend walked across to a cabinet, and took out a small heap of newspapers, from which he selected one. "Where is it? Let me see—h'm! Ah, here! After giving the details of the original calumny, which I needn't repeat to you, the worthy editor proceeds as follows:—'*It is true that our London contemporary was afterwards induced—how, it boots not to inquire—to withdraw this particular charge against the Crown lawyer whom immoral capitalists, renegade Liberals, and unscrupulous Tory agitators have combined to try and foist upon the suffrages of the men of Coln; but we think it only fair and needful that our readers and the electors generally should know in what terms the withdrawal was made. We therefore subjoin the entire paragraph.*

" " " It appears that a statement published last week in this journal" (*Town Talk*) " concerning a certain well-known lawyer and M.P. is unfounded. We desire herewith to express our regret that it should have found its way into this as into other newspapers. But, after all, the honourable and learned gentleman in question has only himself to thank if such rumours obtain too ready credence. He'has been the acknowledged hero of so many tales similar in character to that lately current amongst us, that it need create no surprise in his mind if even logical and sober-minded persons are occasionally, as in the present instance, led astray in their conclusions by a too close consideration of mere probabilities. There are possible drawbacks, as the brilliant member for Coln is perhaps beginning to discover, to the enviable but peculiar fame which attends a social career like his—stinging whips which the gods are pleased to fashion for our scourging out of our pleasant vices. One of the most galling of these consists in the awkward retentiveness of some people's memories, and the unwelcome advent on the scene of old acquaintances who, just when we are masquerading most successfully in the livery of virtue, insist on hailing us as one of the wicked."

"'*Thus the Editor of* Town Talk. *We commend his reflections to the serious and unbiased consideration of the brave and righteous men of Coln. In reproducing them we have only fulfilled an imperative duty, having no desire to inflict personal pain upon Mr. Wentworth or his friends. Mr. Wentworth has recently suffered domestic bereavement of a painful kind; and if, as has been credibly reported to us by some who should have had good opportunity of knowing the truth, the fatal termination of an illness which all united in deploring was not improbably accelerated by the perusal of the story in question, a certain amount of punishment has already been meted out to one who is the worthy agent of a Government equally devoid of feeling and principle, a Government which is now trampling on the dearest rights of man in Wales, in order that it may have its hands free to rivet the fetters of the working-men of England.'* I hope you admire the gratuitous brutality and devilish malignity of those concluding sentences," Colonel Townsend wound up, his handsome face ablaze with indignation.

"Referring to the death of his daughter, I

suppose? Abominable!' muttered Sir John. "But, even supposing this were true, how could they have heard it?"

"Servants," answered Townsend, briefly and suggestively. "These low reporters will push themselves anywhere, and don't care what gutters they fish in, so they hook up the slander required."

"What was done? Did you answer them?"

"Wentworth answered them. By Jove, that man has the pluck of a lion! He positively carried me off my feet for a few minutes that evening, and I thought my days for enthusiasm were over. I'll tell you how it was. The day this scoundrelly attack appeared, Wentworth was going to address a large meeting in the Town Hall. This precious rag is an evening paper, published about six o'clock, so he knew nothing of its last exploit when he appeared on the platform. Owing to disturbances at recent meetings, we had issued tickets for this one, but —by some collusion with one of the doorkeepers, I suppose—an emissary of the other side had made his way in and scattered a number of copies of that day's issue of the *Banner* all about the hall. As Wentworth came to his place, one was handed up to him by somebody, and while the chairman was speaking, he opened and read it. He did not move a muscle, but I saw him turn livid suddenly. 'Good God, Wentworth!' I said, 'what's the matter?' He hesitated a moment, and then turned and put the thing into my hand without a word."

"Truly," said Sir John, who was getting nearly as much interested, if not as excited, as his friend, " it was a test which might well have tried any man's courage!"

Colonel Townsend continued, without heeding the interpolation, " I asked him if he thought his opening the paper had been observed; because, if not, I should advise his quietly ignoring the whole thing for the evening. ' Let us get through this safely,' I said, ' and to-morrow you can write them any reply you like.' For answer, he simply signed to me to look at the body of the hall, and I saw at once that quite a third of the audience had copies of the *Banner* in their hands. My dear Clavering, that was an awful moment! I can tell you I heartily regretted having allowed myself to be drawn into the political whirlpool again."

" Well?" asked Sir John eagerly.

" Well, Wentworth got up. I shall never forget his face as he confronted his hearers—the mingled anguish and fearlessness of it. When he began, in a low clear voice, 'Gentlemen'—the only sign of flurry about him was that he forgot to include the chairman in his address—stay a moment; I have his speech here somewhere."

Colonel Townsend dived again into his cabinet, brought a paper to light, and held it out to the lamp, which he turned up for his own better convenience in reading.

"'Gentlemen,—Before we proceed to the consideration of those national topics on which it is my purpose to address you this evening, it appears necessary that I should speak a few words on a subject purely personal. This is a circumstance which I regret, but as your former representative and as a candidate for your suffrages next week I feel I have no choice left me in the matter. The charges contained in the paper which I hold in my hand, and which I perceive in the hands of a large proportion of those present at this meeting, are such as cannot be passed over in silence. With respect to the slanderous story which is there given in detail, I think it is not needful for me to say much. Its truth was, at the time of its circulation, wholly disproved (cheers), as you will observe that the editor of *Town Talk* himself admits. (Hear, hear, and a voice, "So he does.") That he has chosen to accompany his witness to its falsity by a multitude of other and vaguer insinuations detracts, or should detract, nothing from the value of the testimony itself—perhaps should rather increase its value, as showing plainly that it emanates unwillingly from an avowed and implacable enemy. Gentlemen, the story was false; from first to last a lying and wholly groundless invention. When I add that I make this assertion on the honour of an English gentleman, I have, I trust, said enough. (Loud cheers.)'

("So far, so good," Colonel Townsend commented parenthetically. "The surprise to us all was yet to come.)

"'But the paragraph quoted brings against me an indictment of a larger and more extensive scope. To this indictment you will expect—and you will be fully within your rights in expecting that I should return some kind of reply. And the reply which I return, the only reply which perfect honesty and frankness permits me to return, is that I admit, to a great extent, its truth, although that truth is expressed in a cruel and malignant form. I hold it alike useless and insincere for me to protest to you, an audience of plain working-men, who prefer, I presume, the plain unvarnished truth to any kind of delicate equivocation, that there is not much in my past life on which I look back with deep shame and bitter regret. Of the precise magnitude of my errors, and of the question whether they have been so great as to disqualify me for the work I have endeavoured to do and hoped yet to do again as your representative, it is not for me now to judge, but for you. For my own part, I had cherished a hope—I trust, not a presumptuous one—that my back being finally turned on a past which is my darkest recollection, I might not even now be counted altogether unworthy· to serve my country and my fellow-countrymen in that position which seems to offer me the greatest opportunities of usefulness to both. Your suffrages alone can finally answer this question, as I have said. But I conceive it my duty, considering what has taken place to-night, not to await even their verdict. I shall at once place myself unreservedly in the hands of the National Liberal Committee' (here the speaker made a slight inclination towards the noble chairman), 'and shall be entirely guided by their advice and decision in the matter of further prosecuting my candidature.'

("There was a dead silence after this for a moment; you might literally have heard the traditional pin drop. When Wentworth began again, his voice—which had been quite steady hitherto—became suddenly tremulous, and I was in mortal fear lest he should be going to break down altogether.)

"'There is one allusion, one insinuation, in this article of the *Coln Banner of Right*, on which you will observe that I have refrained from making any comment whatsoever. Its nature is such that I am sure no elector of Coln, be he my political supporter or my most bitter political opponent, will expect me for a moment to dwell upon it. I speak not of its truth or falsehood, which can concern none here; neither do I appeal to the common humanity which its mention has outraged. I hold it unnecessary to do so, since I decline to believe that any man not rendered temporarily insane by political fury could deliberately attempt to excuse, much less justify, the infliction of a wound so horrible on any fellow-man, even were that man his unpardonable foe. The matter itself I refuse to discuss. Questions so awful are best left to a man's own conscience and the Ruler of it. Gentlemen, I have done."

"That was all," Colonel Townsend concluded,

refolding his newspaper. "He turned round, drank a glass of water—in dead silence all the while, for the men seemed too stupefied to cheer —and then turned back again and made the finest speech on the Welsh riots I have heard him make yet. Afterwards he went home and wrote his letter to the committee. So now you know the history of 'The Coln Incident'—and an uncommonly startling incident it was, I can assure you !"

"But what was the result of the affair ?"

"Why, of course we would not accept his proffered resignation—assent to his withdrawal would be the more correct phrase, I suppose. I hope we are none of us too purblind yet to know a man when we see one. If I had felt sure beforehand that it would cost us the seat, I don't think I could have advised the rest to let Wentworth withdraw."

"Then the seat was lost ?"

"Not exactly! My friends the weavers also knew a man when they saw one, apparently. Wentworth was returned by a majority which had leaped up from 29 to 730, and the editor of the *Banner of Right* found it expedient to retire for a space into the valley of silence and seclusion.'

CHAPTER X.

"WHAT I COULD, I DID.'

"... To trace the hidden equities of divine reward, and to catch sight, through the darkness, of the fateful threads of woven fire that connect error with retribution."—RUSKIN.

SUMMER, autumn, winter—all these had come and gone, and another spring was abroad upon the earth.

And if everywhere was to be felt something of the beauty and joyousness of the season, its most riotous beauty and overflowing joyousness seemed to be flung out over the grey university city on the banks of the Isis, where the soft spring breeze was rustling pleasantly among the great branches of the elms in Christ Church Walk, and the river-side meadows were dappled all over with patches of white and yellow—where the quiet gardens of the colleges had suddenly flushed into a thousand colours, and even the ancient walls themselves had grown bright here and there with rainbow hues. Everywhere the time of the singing of birds had come, but nowhere so fully as at Oxford, where the nightingales sang even at noonday in the dark cool recesses of Bagley Wood, and the swallows eddied and circled, twittering gaily, round the battlements of Magdalen Tower, and the homely little sparrow himself chirped more cheerfully than elsewhere, from his fearless perch on some Gothic window-sill.

It was the last week of May, and the beautiful old city had put on her festal robes, ready to rejoice in the manly feats of the youngest of her children at their yearly aquatic contest, and to smile a welcome to those elder sons of hers who returned for a brief season to pay Alma Mater her annual tribute of respect and affection. In a word, it was the week of "the Eights," as they are fondly and familiarly known to Oxford men ; and the Oxonian of the past had come down with his wife and daughters to see how the younger generation comported itself in the struggle in which, ten, twenty, or even thirty years ago, he had himself borne some triumphant part. He is a leading barrister now, our old Oxonian, or a popular preacher, mayhap even a rising statesman, or a distinguished man of letters ; but never will the most flattering article in the *Times* or *Athenæum*, or the sight of a very sea of upturned faces below the pulpit of the metropolitan cathedral, or even the plaudits of an excited House of Commons, thrill him with such a sense of gratified pride as the wild cheers which told him, while the boat in which he held the proud position of stroke glided past the winning-post, that his college was head of the river.

So the queen of universities had her halls and walks and garden glades filled to overflowing, in these last bright days of May, with a more or less motley crowd ; for the throng included a whole galaxy of fashionable idlers from town, who found it pleasant to spend part of the Whitsuntide recess in Oxford. Some few visitors there were who came only for a single day, and among these came Paul Wentworth, escorting his daughter Mabel, who was now nearly eighteen. Since her recent formal introduction into society, Mabel had developed as abnormal an appetite for pleasure of all kinds as could be expected even of her mother's child. Nothing came amiss to her in the shape of amusement, and without amusement of some kind she could not exist, apparently ; so Wentworth found that, if he was not to lose his hold over her affections altogether, he must consent to resume the habits which he had almost wholly laid aside, and cultivate society's good graces for her sake, if not for his own. The task was painful to him beyond words, but he performed it unflinchingly, and counted himself well paid by a careless word of thanks, or a mere expression of selfish gratification even, from Mabel's lips. She was not prodigal of either, it is true; but this made Wentworth value such utterances the more. Only Margaret, watching the shadow which would often steal over her brother's worn face in the midst of his keenest arguments and most brilliant conversational passages-at-arms, guessed the nightly self-sacrifice at the shrine of Mabel's craving for enjoyment, and felt her heart grow hot within her at the unresponsive, passive indifference with which the girl accepted her father's untiring efforts to make her happy. Where Mabel's concerns were in question, Wentworth was never busy, never tired; no exertion was too great for him, no detail too small to evoke his eager interest. All which solicitude and devotion Mabel took very quietly, as no more than her right. Since Wentworth showed himself so desperately anxious to please her, she concluded that it was his one duty in life to do so, and she could perceive no reason for endeavouring to spare him in any way. Even his political obligations, the only calls upon his time ever allowed to interfere with her plans and desires, she resented bitterly, with all a woman's strength of resentment, joined to a child's obstinacy of unreasonableness. Thus she had taken it into her wilful head to spend three days at Oxford, and was sorely chagrined and angered when her father reluctantly announced that he could not possibly spare more than twelve hours from his work at the Welsh Office.

"It is the recess," she murmured rebelliously. "What is the use of a recess if we are tied fast in London all the time?"

"My darling, you don't understand," Wentworth explained patiently. "Departmental work does not stop for the recess. With affairs in Wales in their present condition, it is positively necessary that I should be at my post."

"The other Ministers are away," Mabel persisted. "When the Premier and Lord Ellesthorpe and Mr. Orme can go abroad, surely the Secretary for Wales might take three days at Oxford. And you are not even in the Cabinet."

"No," rejoined Wentworth, forcing a smile.

"Not yet. When I reach that exalted position, perhaps I shall be able to take more holidays. At present I must devote myself to the duties of my humble secretaryship. I am only on trial, as it were, and so is the office itself just now; I have everything to learn, you know. You wouldn't wish the first Welsh Secretary to be pronounced a failure, would you?"—laying a caressing hand on his daughter's shoulder.

She released herself quietly from his hold. "It is all very well to laugh," she replied pettishly, "but it is hard that you will never do anything I ask you, father."

Wentworth's eyes gave one irrepressible angry flash. "Mabel!" he exclaimed reproachfully. Then, checking himself, he added with a kind of weary resignation, "Well, I suppose it is difficult for you to understand these things; perhaps I ought not to expect you to do so. I must repeat that it is impossible, utterly impossible, for me to leave London for three days at present; but I will take you to Oxford for the day either on Tuesday or Wednesday, whichever you prefer."

So on Wednesday, which Mabel fixed upon as the last and most exciting day of the boat-races, she and Wentworth travelled down to Oxford by

an early train. They lunched with Irvine in
his rooms at St. Bride's, where Mabel, who had
a wholesome awe of her uncle, was fain to
conceal the ill temper she made no secret of to
her father, and finally went down to the river
about four o'clock in such a veritable glory of
May sunshine as should have sufficed to dissipate the worst and most settled cloud of girlish
resentment. It was not without its effect even
on Mabel's mood. She unbent visibly as they
rowed leisurely along under the trees that
overhang the Cherwell, and by the time they
reached the Isis itself, and had crossed the
rickety plank bridge which must be passed in
order to gain their coign of vantage on St.
Swithun's barge, her smiles were no longer constrained and joyless.

She was speedily seized upon by a group of
acquaintances, as was Wentworth himself in his
turn, and he saw hardly anything of her for the
rest of the afternoon. Only, in the interval after
the second division races had been rowed, she
came to him and said carelessly, "I am going
with Mrs. St. John to the Christ Church barge
for a change. You will find me there when it is
time to go away."

Wentworth let her go without protest, glad

that she should be happy anywhere and content
even though it were apart from him, for he had
long since resigned himself to the knowledge
that he no longer counted for a factor in the
sum of her happiness. He let her go, stifling a
sigh as she tripped off, and turned his attention
to the scene around and before him—to the
masses and contrasts of colour grouped together
on the long line of barges crowded with well-
dressed women and girls in delicate or bright-
hued summer gowns; to the shifting kaleidoscope
on the opposite bank, where all the colours of
the rainbow were continually crossing and re-
crossing each other like the shuttles in a loom,
as young Oxford, in the various dyes of its legion
boat clubs, cricket clubs, and tennis clubs, ran
excitedly to and fro; to the St. Swithun's men
climbing warily into their outrigger alongside
the barge, while a dozen more such shallow
graceful craft were beginning to make their way
up the smooth stream to the starting-point far
out of sight—the whole moving picture set in
such a frame of emerald meadows dappled with
white and gold, and of majestic trees in the perfection of their spring verdure, and bathed more-
over in such a flood of sparkling sunshine as
might well enchant the eye and heart of a man

whose time for the last five weeks had been divided between harassing despatches, protracted small-hour sittings, and distasteful society, between the atmosphere of the House of Commons and the atmosphere of London drawing-rooms. Wentworth withdrew a little from Irvine and his friends that he might contemplate all this at his ease, possessing himself of a vacant seat which he espied at the back of the barge—vacant, that is, in so far that it was only occupied by a lady's dust-cloak.

He was not long left in possession of the coveted resting-place, however. Not two minutes had elapsed before a figure detached itself from the crowd at the extreme upper end of the barge, where the throng was thickest, and came towards his corner. The owner of the cloak, no doubt, who possibly considered herself the owner of the seat as well. He rose instinctively as the lady approached, and as he did so, perceived that it was Muriel Arlingham.

At the same moment she recognized him, and recognized also that she was too near him already to think of retreating unobserved. There was a slight, an almost imperceptible, hesitation about her for a second; then she moved on and held out her hand.

"How do you do, Mr. Wentworth? Are you staying in Oxford?"

"No, I am only here for the day. I came to bring my daughter," he answered briefly and formally. "I hope you are well?"

"Quite well, thank you. Is your daughter here?" Muriel asked, glancing round inquiringly.

"She is on the Christ Church barge," Wentworth answered, following her glance, "with a party of friends. I am sorry she is not at hand; I should like you to have seen her. She has altered a great deal of late, and grown into a young woman all in a moment."

"Girls do alter very rapidly at her age," Muriel rejoined. "I have heard of her at various times, and every one tells me how pretty she is. Of course I knew she had been presented in March."

"You have not been in town yourself yet this season, I think?" Wentworth said, in as matter-of-fact a tone as he could assume.

"No, nor at all last season. We have been abroad nearly two years, and only returned to England a few days ago. We have been leading rather a desultory life lately. You, on the contrary, have been very full of work; at least, so we judged from the newspapers."

"Yes, I have had plenty to do," he answered.

Muriel wondered whether his work agreed with him. He had certainly aged by ten years rather than two—the actual time which had elapsed since she saw him last in Lord Carlton's library at Graymere—but then, she had always felt persuaded that that day had been the last of his perfect prime of manhood, the death-day of that youthfulness of mind and spirit which had clung to him so long. His face had rather gained than lost in intellectual force, by an extreme thinness which gave more striking prominence to its large outlines and strongly marked features; but its chief characteristic now seemed to Muriel its settled patience of expression—a patience almost terrible in its fixedness, eloquent as it was of perpetual suffering and perpetual endurance. That look, Muriel knew instinctively, Paul Wentworth would carry with him to his grave.

"I may congratulate you on having joined the Ministry, I suppose?" she said a little timidly. "We were very glad to read of your appointment last February." Wentworth noticed that she was careful to use the plural pronoun in speaking of her interest in his affairs, thus associating herself with her husband.

"Thank you," he replied. "The appointment

must have been a great surprise to you, no doubt, as it was to most people, and above all to myself. There seemed to be many reasons why office should *not* be offered to me; but the times are difficult, and I suppose pressing needs outweighed considerations of expediency."

Muriel, who had read the history of the Coln election, like every one else, could easily guess what thought underlay Wentworth's words. She answered more hastily than was usual with her, "Yours is no light undertaking at present, unhappily; but already things seem to be on the mend in Wales. If you can succeed in reintroducing order there, it will indeed be matter for rejoicing."

"It is a great 'If,'" Wentworth replied rather sadly. "The outbreak at Broom-y-Clos last week was not a very encouraging token of success, I fear."

"It was an isolated outbreak," Muriel rejoined with something of her old eagerness. "After all, the great thing is to be moving on the right lines."

"Ah! as to that, I am quite confident," Wentworth answered her. "Whatever the errors of Government in the Welsh business heretofore, they have laid down the right principle now, and are acting on it. Had I not felt convinced of this, I would never have accepted office. As to the results of my administration, I am not over sanguine; but that is not my business." He looked full at Muriel, with eyes in which the old unshaken fearlessness still reigned, but tempered and softened now by a touch of sorrowful humility. "I believe that it is worse than useless to try and escape the consequences of past errors, however earnestly and honestly you may try to repair the errors themselves. The law is the same for men and nations, and we can only do our best and accept our punishment." His lips quivered slightly. "I do my best," he added, as simply as a child might have said it.

A light flashed over Muriel's face and died away again, leaving, nevertheless, a radiant trace of its passage behind. The only real happiness she might ever know on earth had been given her by Wentworth's words. Since things were thus with him, she could be well content.

She took up her cloak, and turned to go back to her former station. "Good-bye," she said gently but resolutely. "If my husband should pass presently, will you kindly tell him where to find me up there? I have been expecting him for some time; he has been lunching with friends at the Randolph, and told me to meet him here more than two hours ago. So I came with my cousin, Mr. Osborne, who is pulling bow in the St. Swithun boat. Mr. Arlingham must have been detained in some way; I cannot think what has become of him."

"I will tell him, certainly." In his heart he was asking furiously what Arlingham could be about to desire his fair young wife to come and meet him, and then fail to keep his appointment, leaving her alone in so public a place. And what did that look mean, that look of uneasiness almost amounting to fear, which crossed Muriel's face when speaking of her husband's absence?

CHAPTER XI.

ORDEAL BY FIRE.

"It may be the height of courage to say 'I dare not,' and the height of love to say 'I will not.'"—BISHOP STUBBS.

WENTWORTH'S questionings were destined to receive a speedy answer. About ten minutes after Muriel had left him, he saw her husband stroll up to the steps of the St. Swithun's barge and climb rather heavily on board.

Wentworth regarded the young man critically. Arlingham, too, had altered a good deal during the past two years, and altered for the worse. His dress was of a pronouncedly "horsey" character, and there was a strong suggestion of the turf and the betting ring about his whole appearance; his face, too, was flushed, and his blue eyes — still his chief beauty — looked unnaturally bright. He had evidently, Wentworth decided, taken quite as much champagne as was good for him during that prolonged luncheon at the Randolph; and though he was still quite in possession of his senses, he was just sufficiently excited to talk a little louder, laugh a little more boisterously, and stare about him with rather more freedom than was perfectly consonant with gentleman-like good manners. Wentworth's hand clenched itself in a mingled passion of loathing, dismay, and frantic apprehension, as he watched him proceed leisurely towards the upper end of the barge, evidently in search of Muriel, followed by his companion. For Arlingham was not alone; and if anything could have increased Wentworth's indignation and distress, it would have been the sight of this companion of his—a well-known professional betting man of more than doubtful reputation, with whom all the higher stamp of racing men had long before refused to have any dealings, and on whom even the more respectable bookmakers were in the habit of looking askance. What in the name of Heaven did Arlingham mean by bringing such a blackguard to a college barge, and into the company of ladies, including his own wife? Good heavens! Wentworth was on his feet as if he had been struck. Arlingham was introducing the man to Muriel, and he was coolly taking a seat by her side.

The bookmaker, who had no doubt indulged quite as freely in the Randolph champagne as his host, appeared to feel no awkwardness in his unaccustomed position, but laughed and chatted with an air of easy familiarity which in Wentworth's eyes seemed to border very closely on insolence; while Muriel, plainly shrinking from his neighbourhood, gave brief cold answers that failed altogether of their purpose in checking his advances towards acquaintance. She made a gesture of appeal to her husband, but he disregarded it, and went forward with the crowd to the rail of the barge, over which all who could reach it were now leaning eagerly, since it wanted but a few minutes of the hour fixed for the first division boats' start.

It only needed that irrepressible token of dislike and fear on Muriel's part to decide Wentworth's course of action. Since there was no one else to protect her, he must do so. He stepped quickly forward, and touched a man standing near him on the arm.

"Townsend," he said rapidly, as the person he addressed turned round in surprise, "will you do me a great service?"

"Surely, my dear fellow, if I can. What is it?"

"In your career on the turf, did you ever come across a bookmaker named Whetstone?"

"I knew him by name and by sight; I took good care never to know him in any other way. A consummate scoundrel, if ever one stepped! What of him?"

"He is here, on this barge," Wentworth said breathlessly. "The man who had the effrontery to bring him here has introduced him to a lady of my acquaintance, and I can see that he is annoying her. I want to rid her of him quietly —without doing anything to attract people's attention, you understand?—especially as I don't think the fellow is quite sober. May I say that you want to speak to him for a moment? Ask him a few questions, and keep him in play for five minutes if you can, will you?" He turned away, hardly waiting to hear his friend's words of ready acquiescence, and the next minute he was standing before Muriel and the bookmaker.

"Pardon me," he said, lifting his hat with punctilious politeness to the latter, "for interrupting you; but a friend of mine—Colonel Townsend—is particularly anxious to speak to you on a matter of pressing business. Will you give him a few minutes' interview? You will find him over there "— signing in the direction

of Colonel Townsend, who stood a little apart
from the rest of the crowd.

"I'm not doing business to-day," the man
answered rather insolently. "I'll wait upon the
Colonel some other time, if he pleases, with
pleasure. This isn't a day for business, is it,
Mrs. Arlingham?" he demanded, appealing to
Muriel in a familiar tone which made Wentworth's blood boil.

He was almost beside himself with passion,
but he preserved his composure admirably.
"Colonel Townsend's business is of the utmost
importance," he repeated, "and he is leaving
Oxford for the north this same evening. I must
beg you"—here Wentworth fixed his eyes on
Whetstone in such a manner that that worthy
quailed beneath them—"I must really beg you
most earnestly to comply with his request. In
view of the unusual circumstances, this lady will,
I am sure, excuse you readily."

A faint "Certainly," from Muriel.

"Well, if I must, I must, I suppose," said the
bookmaker sulkily, rising slowly and reluctantly
to his feet. "I'll be back presently." He looked
as if he would have liked to add something more,
but that steady, overmastering gaze of Wentworth's cowed him into silence. He moved away
without further remark.

Then Muriel looked up to Wentworth with a passion of gratitude in her eyes. "What shall I do?" she said appealingly. "I must go home."

"You are ill," Wentworth asserted abruptly, for she was trembling from head to foot, and every vestige of colour had left her face. Even her lips were livid in their deadly whiteness.

She did not deny his assertion. "I must go home," she repeated, half rising. Wentworth motioned her back into her seat.

"Not this moment," he replied in a brief, business-like way. "Wait till the gun has gone off for the start: then no one will pay any attention to you. You can hold on for a few minutes longer, I am sure." He looked at his watch. "It is just past the hour now."

One minute—two minutes—three—then came the sound of a distant report. Wentworth replaced his watch and took up Muriel's cloak. "There it is," he said composedly. "Now come."

Muriel rose obediently.

"Go straight on downstairs," Wentworth continued in the same tone of quiet command, "and I will join you. I have to speak to my brother first, but I shall be with you instantly; you will not have to wait."

He kept his word to the letter. By the time that Muriel, with the help of the hand-rail, had reached *terra firma*, he had issued his brief instructions to Irvine, and was again by her side.

"Mr. Wentworth," she said helplessly, trying to support herself by putting one hand on an old broken post close by, "I am very sorry—but I am afraid—I am going to faint——"

"Before all these people?" said Wentworth severely. "You will please do nothing of the kind; and you need not if you exert yourself. You can walk across that bridge and round the first bend of the Cherwell perfectly well if you try. I shall not even give you my arm."

The salutary sharpness had its effect—the effect which Wentworth intended it to have. Pale, cold, tremulous, nearly blind, with her heart throbbing in her ears and her limbs almost refusing to do their office, Muriel did nevertheless manage to drag herself across the swaying planks and to struggle a few steps further by the Cherwell, until the first friendly winding of the path took her out of sight of the barges. Then she sank down on a bench which was happily at hand, utterly exhausted. "I shall be better presently," she faintly said. "This is just a faintness from my heart. I have it occasionally if—— "

" I know," he said hastily—and his voice was marvellously changed. But he instantly resumed his former tone again, saying, " Give me your handkerchief to dip in the water, and then put it on your head. Hadn't you better take off your hat ? You can do it for yourself, can't you ? You need not mind; no one will come this way at present. Let me put your cloak behind you to lean against—so. Now I would recommend you to keep quiet for a few minutes."

Muriel obeyed his orders implicitly, one after another, and then remained leaning back motionless, in silence broken only by the faint sounds of distant cheering on the river bank, while he stood quietly on the gravel path beside her. A certain sense of restfulness, born partly of extreme momentary weakness and partly due to a consciousness of Wentworth's watchful protection, stole over her. Had her companion spoken a single word, however kind or sympathizing, such a word would have jarred upon her; but his silent presence was a source of strength in itself.

At last Wentworth, seeing the colour begin to return to her cheeks, felt constrained to break the silence. "Are you better?" he asked. But he did not put the question with much eagerness. It occurred to him whether for Muriel herself it might not have been happier had she failed to recover so easily. To have had her slip quietly away out of life altogether, instead of coming back to it to face such a future as he foresaw for her, would have been the least painful fate that could befall her, to Wentworth's mind.

She looked up, startled out of the semi-conscious dream into which she had drifted, and almost expecting to find herself in the rough shepherd's hut of seven years earlier, and see Wentworth standing in the doorway with the glamour of those days about him still. But she bore the shock of her sudden return to bitter reality very calmly. "I am much better," she declared. "Indeed, I feel almost well now."

"That's right," Wentworth answered, with resolute cheerfulness. "They have stopped cheering now, so people will soon be moving off. If you feel equal to it, therefore, I think we had better be going too. Can you walk, do you think?"

"Oh yes!" Muriel answered confidently. But no sooner had her feet touched the ground than another wave of deadly faintness swept over her. "I don't believe I can," she ejaculated despairingly. "What am I to do? There is no possibility of driving."

Wentworth inwardly cursed the folly of the university authorities, or the Town Council, or whatever local body was responsible for leaving the approaches to the river without a carriage road. "Where are you staying?" he asked.

"With my cousin, Miss Bretherton. She has taken a house near the Parks—in Ridley Gardens."

"That solves the difficulty, then. The Cherwell is navigable as far as Ridley Gardens, I know; and I can row you up in my brother's boat, which we left close by. 1 will have it here in a moment."

So it came to pass that, in a few minutes, Muriel found herself seated once more in the stern of a boat, with Wentworth opposite to her. But they did not talk, as they would have done in the old days. She was still feeling ill enough to have a good excuse for silence; and he devoted his whole attention to keeping the little craft he directed clear of the banks of the narrow stream, and avoided even looking at his companion.

It was she who spoke at last. "I wonder if

my husband will be alarmed at my strange disappearance ?" she said, with an odd little laugh. "I ought to have told him I was going home."

"You need not be uneasy," Wentworth answered gravely. "I thought of that, and left a message with my brother for him. Philip said he would find him out, and I dare say they will walk home together."

Muriel's eyes gave a curious flash. "If they do, I fear they will bore each other terribly," she observed. "Your brother is a most admirable man, Mr. Wentworth, but I am afraid his improving discourses will hardly go down with Mr. Arlingham and his friends; he is a little too high-flown for ordinary people. My husband would probably imagine that he was being taken to task or instructed, and there are few things he dislikes so much. Most men share that feeling."

"I don't think Phil is at all likely to commit such a strategical mistake," Wentworth replied lightly, taking no notice of Muriel's sudden resentful bitterness. "If he were in the habit of making such blunders, he would not have so many friends left among his old pupils. Did you know, by the way, that Mr. Arlingham had been a pupil of his once ?"

" I knew he had coached with him for a short time. But my husband gave more of his time at the university to boating than to books— which, I am sure, must have been a great source of annoyance to his late tutor. Doesn't your brother consider the river more or less of a snare to Young Oxford ? "

Again Wentworth deliberately ignored the singular tone of Muriel's remarks. " No, I believe he is all in favour of plenty of physical exercise," he rejoined. " He would be glad to introduce it among his East Enders, if only he could get the necessary space wherein they might disport themselves. Do we land here, at the end of this road ? "

" No ; my cousin has a landing-place at the bottom of her garden, just round the corner." And two or three more vigorous strokes of Wentworth's sculls brought them to the half-dozen steps which led down from Miss Brether-ton's sunny, well-kept lawn to the Cherwell.

Wentworth made the boat fast, and Muriel sprang out with a great show of agility. But once on land, it was plain that she still trembled so much that she could scarcely walk, and that she was trusting partly to the stick of her sun-shade for support. Nevertheless, Wentworth did not offer to help her, judging that she would prefer to remain unassisted; he only followed watchfully behind her, carrying her cloak, and happily the way across the lawn and up a smoothly gravelled path, between newly planted flower-beds, to the house was not long or fatiguing. Muriel did not go round to the front door, which was on the other side of the pretty, semi-ecclesiastical looking building, but went straight in at the open French window of the drawing-room, and sat down on the sofa. Wentworth quietly laid down the cloak he carried.

"Perhaps, after feeling so faint, it would be well if you had some tea, or something of that kind, wouldn't it?" he inquired almost timidly. "Would you like me to ring for your maid?"

"She is a luxury I have dispensed with," Muriel answered, in the same hard, defiant tone she had used in the boat—a tone utterly new to Wentworth from her lips. "I have gone back to Spartan simplicity in my domestic arrangements lately. However, Miss Bretherton's maid would have answered the bell if you had rung it; but I don't feel any particular craving for tea, thank you. I only want a little salutary quiet now to recover myself perfectly."

Wentworth turned a shade paler, but did not

permit himself to betray the slightest annoy-ance. "Very likely you are quite right," he replied. "I dare say an hour or two's rest will quite restore you. I can therefore the more easily ask you to excuse me at once, as I have to meet my daughter in time to go to Christ Church for half an hour before we leave for town. Good-bye. I trust you will soon feel altogether yourself again."

She let him touch her hand and utter his formal farewell while she sat still, thanklessly silent in the agony of wounded pride, which for a few minutes had made her like another woman. But when he actually turned away, she knew that she could not let him go thus. "Mr. Wentworth," she exclaimed, rising to her feet, "forgive me that I have not—that I *cannot* thank you for what you have done for me to-day. Forgive me, please, as you pity me."

He turned back, his eyes suddenly soft with tears. "My dear child," he said very gently, "there is nothing for me to forgive, nor any reason why you should thank me. As an old acquaintance, I thought I might venture to try and be of service to you under circumstances that were a little annoying—that was all!"

"All!" she repeated. "You were generous,

thoughtful, considerate beyond words—and I repaid you almost with insults. I tried to wound you because you had helped me. You cannot think more hardly of me than I do of myself. Why should I be too proud to bear your pity ? "

" I do not think," Wentworth answered rather unsteadily, "that pity, mixed with so much honour and reverence as mine is, need hurt you."

" Everything hurts me to-day," she said hopelessly. " Kindness, I think, most of all. Consider me mad for the moment, if you like, only don't think me ungrateful ! "

" There is no question of ingratitude here," Wentworth replied ; " I understand you perfectly. You should not try a man beyond his strength," he added, half below his breath.

But Muriel neither heard nor heeded his last words. " You are mistaken if you think you understand," she returned ; " it is impossible that you should. And please do not be sympathetic. If there is a thing I shrink from on earth, it is sympathy ! "

She *had* tried him beyond his strength. Paul Wentworth had known many fierce temptations in his life, but never so fierce a one as that which assailed him at this moment. He took two or three hasty steps about the room, and finally came over and stood before her. "Muriel," he said hoarsely, "is our fate going to be too strong for us, after all?"

She shrank together suddenly. "No—oh no!" she ejaculated faintly. "Surely, surely not."

"I think it seems so," Wentworth replied, with a kind of desperate calm. "We have done our best, we have struggled against this with all our strength—you know it—and what is the result to us both? I appeal to you. You have striven for years to be a perfectly true and loyal wife to that man—I will not speak of him, because he is your husband—and to-day you had your reward. According to my imperfect fashion—a very different one from yours, but it was the best I could do, and I did it honestly—I have struggled also. That conflict is over now, as far as I am concerned."

She did not interrupt him, she did not contradict him. She only turned away a little, and stood looking out through the open window. "Why should you despair?" she said falteringly. "It is only the old miserable story——"

"No, it is not only that," Wentworth broke in. "After what has happened to-day, nothing is or an be the same. Am I calmly to leave you to a repetition of this afternoon's scene, or worse ? It will be worse, as time goes on; common experience tells you that it must be worse. Can you expect a man to whom you are the most precious thing on earth to acquiesce quietly in such a fate for you? I neither can nor will acquiesce in it. Hitherto I have kept silence, but now that I see what a life lies before you, now that it is too late to hope for anything else, it seems as if even what I could give——"

He broke off abruptly, but a voice at his ear whispered, " *Go on. Go on,*" it said : " *what are you hesitating for? For conscience and righteousness' sake? A likely story—from you ! You know that if you do stop short now, it is simply for the sake of your ambition, to safeguard your political career, and for fear your newly whitewashed name should be freshly blackened in the world's eyes. You are not in the least conscientious: you are only rankly selfish. It is not a choice between good and evil, it is a choice between this woman and yourself——*"

But Muriel had turned slowly round from the window, and was facing him, deadly pale. " I will not believe it is too late," she said. " It is only because I am so wounded and bruised and humiliated that I cannot see right from wrong for the moment. But the power to see will come back—it will come back! I am sure it will. Only you must help me now, while I have no strength at all."

"I am yours—for everything," Wentworth answered impetuously. "I can love and care for you, at least——"

Muriel put up her hand to silence him. "Hush, don't say that!" she implored. "Don't you see that it is the one thing I cannot bear? To be loved, to be cared for, to have done with terrors and conflicts and scruples—don't you see that it may seem a sort of Paradise to me? For the moment—only for the moment, I know. I am mad to-day, but to-morrow I shall have got back to my reason. Till then, help me!"

"How?" he asked. "Have I not said——"

Again Muriel checked the words on his lips: her voice took a ring of passionate appeal. "You see how weak I am; I cannot prevent your seeing it. You see that I am broken-hearted and almost desperate; that I would do anything if I could only forget myself—and be loved a little. But I trust you. Because you know that I cannot bear to hear even once more what you said a moment ago—just because you know that I was *glad* to hear you say it, therefore——"

There was a brief pause before Wentworth answered : a pause of a few seconds only. Then he very quietly completed Muriel's broken sentence. "*Therefore,*" he said, "I will never say it again. Never—so help me God !"

He had indeed faltered dangerously and stumbled heavily, but he had not fallen so far as to be incapable of recovering his lost standing ground. "For what I have said too much already," he added, after a minute, "I can only ask very sorrowfully your forgiveness."

Muriel leaned her head against the window frame, and covered her face with her hands. "I knew—you would see——" she said brokenly. Her tears were dropping fast and silently.

Wentworth looked at her with an unspeakable grief and compassion which had nothing of self left in it. No one could help her, he knew well, and least of all he himself, who dared not even attempt to utter a word of comfort, or lay so much as a pitying touch on that bowed head for a moment. She must carry her own burden, and carry it alone to the end.

"Promise me one thing," he said at last; "promise me, Muriel, that you will not stay with him any longer. You have those who love you, and a home—go back to them and to it. He has lost all right to expect you to stay, and you can do nothing for his happiness—if you are still anxious to sacrifice yourself to that."

She raised her startled face. "Oh, I could not leave him!" she answered. "You forget the wrong I have done and am doing him. My only clear duty is to make what reparation I can. Now, too, when he is poor and unhappy—it is in great measure his misfortunes which are making him so different, so different to what he once was——" Tears would not let her say more.

"You are hard on me," Wentworth said. "Do you think nothing of what I must suffer henceforward?"

"I have no right to think of you," she answered simply. "He is my husband."

"For your own sake—I did wrong to ask that you should remember anything else—for your own sake, then——"

"We will not speak of that further, please," Muriel interposed. Wentworth's decision seemed to have given her back in an instant all her own lost steadfastness. "My mind is made up."

"Can nothing be done?" he asked passionately. "Why should you be condemned to such a fate? Even I have Mabel and my work left me. I have something to live for, if not to make life worth living, while you—you have nothing."

"You are mistaken; I have my duty. That ought to be enough for me always, and by-and-by will be, perhaps. You must not think of me as you have seen me to-day; that darkness does not come often. I am glad it has passed now, before I have to say good-bye to you for the last time. For I think we must not meet again, even as acquaintances, now."

"I suppose not," Wentworth acquiesced heavily. " And—there is nothing I can do for you, now or ever?"

"Nothing," she answered steadily. " Except to go on fulfilling my ideals, as you have been doing of late. You know my old craving after fulfilled ideals. I would like to think you were happier, that is all. Good-bye." A faint smile, which had a touch of victorious satisfaction in it for all its pathos, parted her lips for a moment. " My love to Mabel," she added.

Wentworth held her proffered hand silently in his, looking into her sad face an instant longer—then he let it drop without a word. Since there was nothing he could do for her, now or ever, of what further use were any words between them ?

Passing down the garden on his way to his boat, he encountered Miss Bretherton, looking as trim, light, and energetic as usual. Despising boat-races, she had been attending a lecture given by the Professor of Music, and carried an armful of notebooks. He stopped to greet her and explain his presence in her demesne.

Miss Bretherton's response was of the coldest. She had met Wentworth in London some years earlier, and had formed one of her unaccountable antipathies to him ; and this antipathy had subsequently been abundantly justified to her mind by certain narratives retailed to her by her friend, Lady Clavering. Her manner by no means softened when Wentworth informed her that Mrs. Arlingham had felt faint in the course of the afternoon, and had allowed herself to be escorted home by him. For all his habit of self-command, he could not altogether repress certain evidences of recent agitation, even while he narrated in a matter-of-fact fashion the details of what had taken place on the river, and expressed his regret that Mrs. Arlingham's sudden attack of faintness should have obliged her to leave the St. Swithun's barge at the most interesting moment of the day; and Helen Bretherton's quick suspicions were aroused at sight of this ill-concealed emotion. From that hour forward she was· Paul Wentworth's bitter and implacable enemy.

CHAPTER XII.

VALE!

> "Under another heaven,
> In lands where neither love nor memory
> Can plant a selfish hope—in lands so far
> I should not seem to see the outstretched arms
> That seek me, or to hear the voice that calls,
> I should feel distance only and despair;
> So rest for ever from the thought of bliss,
> And wear my weight of life's great chain unstruggling."
>
> GEORGE ELIOT.

IT is recorded of one of the heroines of an American novel that she was seized on a memorable occasion with an unwonted fit of silence and abstraction, after which she proceeded to address the assembled company—rather a numerous one, by the way—as follows:—"Do you know that I actually have serious thoughts sometimes? I think that very likely some of us—most of us—are going to the dogs. And I wonder what it will be when we get there!"

Had Jack Arlingham been as frank and out-spoken as this New England maiden, he might fitly have employed her utterance to describe his own state of mind. Muriel's husband, too, had an uneasy consciousness that he was "going to the dogs" at an extremely rapid rate; and that the goal towards which he was making such striking progress would prove highly undesirable, he strongly suspected—so his "serious thoughts" served to make him tolerably uncomfortable. There, however, his self-communings stopped short. He had never inquired with sufficient closeness into the nature of the road he was travelling to be thoroughly convinced of the pro-bable and, indeed, inevitable ruin that awaited him not very much further on, much less to become persuaded that the only chance for him lay in turning right round in his course, and trying a fresh departure altogether; therefore, he still allowed himself to be drawn onwards, although with a miserable fear upon him. The intense indolence of nature which had been his curse through life became doubly his curse now. He so hated the trouble of thinking at any time, especially about anything disagreeable; and it cannot be denied that repenting and beginning anew—particularly in debt and poverty, when one has been long accustomed to luxury and credit—is an eminently disagreeable and fatiguing business. Then Arlingham had his share of pride, and his downfall before the world galled him cruelly. Since his return to England, he had become convinced that all hope of living at Eversleigh must be abandoned for so long a period that it no longer seemed even worth while disputing whether the terms of the lease which handed it over to the present tenant should be enlarged to twenty-one, or cut down to fourteen years—and this was the last and bitterest drop in the bitter cup of humiliation that he had mixed for himself. If he could have kept up his old home, he would still have felt that he retained in some measure his old standing among men ; but since Eversleigh was gone, all was gone, and unless some sudden turn of fortune, such as he was always hoping and scheming for, occurred to give him back what he had lost, all that remained to Jack in life was to amuse himself as best he could. The taste for amusement, unnaturally repressed in his boyhood and early youth, had grown almost insatiable since his accession to fortune, and to consequent independence.

Regarding his wife and her feelings on the

matter, Arlingham manifested the most complete indifference. She never troubled him with complaints or reproaches; and, if people do not complain, the most obvious as well as the most convenient conclusion is, that they have nothing to complain of. Since Muriel could accommodate herself with such perfect ease, and absence even of remark, to the altered circumstances of her life, it was natural to suppose that the alteration did not affect her deeply—Jack not being one of those over-sympathetic souls who are fond of divining unspoken sorrows. If you wished to bring your grievances to Mr. Arlingham's notice, it was needful to put them into words and press them on his attention in an audible tone of voice, otherwise he was apt to conclude that no grievance could possibly exist—at any rate, he carefully refrained from making any inquiries on the subject. Which deliberate bridling of his curiosity showed undoubted wisdom on his part; for though he was happily callous to silent and unobtrusive suffering, he would have disliked excessively such suffering becoming vocal and forcing itself on his observation—a catastrophe which might easily have resulted from injudicious questioning.

Indifferent and unsympathetic as Arlingham

was, however, he knew that he had well-nigh passed the limits of his wife's forbearance that fatal afternoon on the St. Swithun's barge. Muriel's cold, grave manner made him aware of this, deepening a certain sense of shame on the subject of his own conduct which had come upon him unbidden as soon as Irvine had fulfilled Wentworth's instructions by giving him a simple message to the effect that "Mrs. Arlingham was feeling overtired, and had therefore decided to go home without waiting for the race to be over." In the light of the next morning what he had done looked even more unpardonable; and all the gentlemanlike instinct which remained latent in him urged him to make apology for it. He was neither fiend nor ruffian; only a very weak, vain, and intensely selfish young man.

As good fortune would have it, he found his wife alone in Miss Bretherton's morning-room, that lady having gone out on one of her many missions of usefulness, charity, or self-improvement. Muriel, who looked very pale and fragile, was writing a letter on foreign paper, but she just glanced up as her husband made his entrance.

"I have copied those instructions for Rogers you spoke to me about on Tuesday," she said. "You will find them on the mantelpiece."

"Thank you. I'm awfully obliged." He felt rather less softened towards her when he saw how she was occupied, wondering instantly if she were writing a graphic account of his misdeeds to her sister—a suspicion the very occurrence of which to his mind showed how little he understood her real nature. However, he had come to say a certain thing, and he meant to say it. "I hope you are better this morning, Muriel," he remarked awkwardly, after moving about the room a little.

"I am much better, thanks. I have rather a bad headache, that is all." There was relenting already in Muriel's tone; it was so rare for her husband to show any evidence of interest in her at all, that his inquiry quite touched her.

"I'm afraid that brute Whetstone's manner annoyed you yesterday," Jack went on more awkwardly still. "I'm sorry now I introduced him to you; perhaps I ought not to have done it."

"I did not like his manner, certainly," Muriel replied. "It would have been better if he had not come to such a place at all, I think."

"As it's my college barge, I imagine I'm the best judge as to the people I can take there with propriety," Jack retorted sullenly. "And I've no doubt he meant to be as civil to you as he knew how. However, I'm sorry I made him known to you, as you didn't like it. Of course you couldn't be expected to like *him*"—Jack felt himself very magnanimous here—"I don't ask it of you. He's a coarse sort of fellow, whom no lady would be likely to take a fancy to. But he asked particularly to be introduced, and as I'm doing a good deal of business with him just now, I thought it best not to refuse him."

"Jack!" Muriel cried, startled out of her usual self-possession. "You are not in his power in any way, surely?"

"Who said I was in his power? How you run off at a tangent, and wrest a man's words, as women always do! Because I may feel it my best policy to keep a man in good humour, does it necessarily follow that he can smash me if he chooses? Do have a little common sense, Muriel!"

"I had no wish to wrest your words," said Muriel, trembling slightly, "but I was startled for the moment by them. I have grown nervous, I suppose," she added, with a pathetic attempt to smile.

Jack was touched in spite of himself. "Poor girl!" he said, touching her arm half caressingly.

"I am sorry if you were upset yesterday. And why I should have given in to Whetstone's cheek, I am sure I don't know. Whatever he does, he can't prevent things going utterly to the bad now. If I could have held on at Eversleigh, indeed——" He turned away his head for a moment.

"I know it is hard to have to let Eversleigh," Muriel said gently. All bitterness had gone out of her; she felt only a great compassion for Jack now. "One can only hope that we may be able to go back there before so very many years are over. Of course I don't know the details of your affairs, but I fancy that might be done, with care and self-denial. I, at least, will do my best for it."

Jack shook his head. "You know nothing about it," he said. But he did not speak unkindly.

"Meanwhile," Muriel continued, "have you thought of any plan for the future? Of where we had better go when we leave this, I mean? We cannot stay very much longer with Helen, you know."

"I have no wish to stay a moment longer with Helen than Helen wishes to keep me," Jack replied, with sudden offence. "You told me she was greatly attached to you, and she was certainly pressing in her invitations."

"She was, indeed," said poor Muriel. "And she will be delighted for us to stay on a while longer. Only eventually, you know, we must set to work to think——"

"It does not take much thinking," Jack interrupted roughly. "There is only one thing to be done, and that is to go abroad again."

The colour sprang into Muriel's face. She had determined to make one last effort for a future that should be better than the past. "Is that necessary?" she asked appealingly.

"I haven't looked at the question in that light. It is simply the only tolerable life for a man with my present wretched means."

"But it is such a terribly unsatisfactory life!" Muriel pleaded eagerly. "Wandering about from place to place—with no home and no real friends. You know you got thoroughly tired of it before; and then you had none of the country life you like, no occupation and no sport. I remember your telling me you only went to Monte Carlo because you were so dreadfully weary of Florence. Now, living quietly in England, we could really manage on less money than we spend in travelling about."

"Living in some abominable suburb in a semi-detached seven-roomed house, perhaps we could."

"No, no; I did not mean anything of that kind! But supposing we were to take some small house in the country, a kind of hunting-box perhaps, in the valley of the Thames? Not a river-side house, for that would be too expensive, I suppose; but one near enough for you to get some boating and fishing in the summer, which you always like. And if we were economical—I would try to be very economical indeed—you might manage to rent a little winter shooting. Surely that would be better than going abroad?"

"No, I don't think it would be at all better," Jack responded. "You forget that a man does not care to live in a wilderness. Economy and fishing are all very well, but a little companionship would not come amiss occasionally. You can read all day, you see; but I don't exactly care for that sort of vegetable existence."

"You could have your friends down to see you in a quiet way—real friends would not mind encountering a little dulness; and I would try to be more sympathetic and cheerful, and make you happier." She rose from the table, and came and leant her trembling hands on his shoulder. "Dear, I am afraid I have not always been to you all that a wife should be, in sympathy and unselfishness; but try this plan, and see if I will not think of you, and you only, henceforward in everything!"

"You are very keen on your plan," Jack said, with a faint sneer. He was not altogether unmoved by his wife's entreaties, but nevertheless he did not mean to yield to them, and, being desirous of silencing her, could think of no way of doing it save by downright rudeness. "You might as well mention your real reason for being so very anxious to stay in England and live in the valley of the Thames. I think there must be something beyond my enjoyment concerned."

Muriel grew paler than ever, but she forced back the indignant words that rushed to her lips. Her recent discovery of her own perilous weakness—she who had always felt herself so strong before!—had filled her with such an agony of self-reproach and self-distrust as quenched resentment before it was well kindled. Perhaps all this was part of her punishment for her yesterday's sin.

"You are wrong there," she said very tremulously. "I was thinking only of you, though not only of your enjoyment. Jack, you know all the miserable outcome of our last stay abroad—— "

" I know that luck has been most cursedly against me for the last two years, both at home and abroad," Jack interposed moodily. " However, I suppose it is bound to turn some day. Meanwhile, if I am to live in genteel poverty, I'm not going to do it next door to my own place. On that point my mind is made up. You would probably get uncommonly tired of a cottage in the country yourself before three months were over : I should not be able to talk literature to you all day like Cunningham, or discuss State affairs with you à la Wentworth. By the way," added Jack, who, like many weak men when they want to back themselves up in a decision, was purposely working himself into a passion, " I congratulate you on your latest admirer, Muriel. For a lady who sets up so high a standard, I must say you don't choose very high-minded friends. I don't go in for exaltation personally, but I fancy I might quite shine as a saint beside Wentworth, if I tried."

Muriel's white lips moved, but made no audible sound. Arlingham was half frightened at the expression on her face.

" You need not look as if I had said something

unpardonable," he ejaculated irritably, his fear showing itself as fear in small natures is apt to do—namely, in an outburst of petulance. "You may have as many admirers as you please, for aught I care. Only don't worry me again about staying in England, because I won't do it; at least, not till I can live at home like a gentleman."

And Muriel never "worried" her husband again on that, or indeed on any subject. After what had passed between them, she recognized finally the utter fruitlessness of such efforts on her part.

One petition only did she subsequently prefer: that when Jack went to London to make arrangements for their final departure from England, she might remain behind at Oxford with her cousin. "I would far rather not go," she urged timidly, "if you have no objection to going without me."

"But I have an objection," Jack answered surlily. "I shall probably want you." He had been dining with a party of friends at one of the river-side hotels, and from various causes had returned home in no pleasant mood. "It is your business to go, and you have no good reason for staying behind. If you had one, you could state it."

"Cannot you imagine that I might wish to avoid meeting people?" she asked, flushing.

"You need not meet people more in London than in Oxford—except those you wish to meet," Jack said, with a disagreeable laugh. "You had better not persist further in this whim of yours, Muriel, or perhaps I shall think the reason you don't give is *not* a good one."

Muriel looked at him steadfastly with her great sad eyes. "If you were quite yourself this evening, Jack," she said, with pathetic dignity, "you would never have said that to me. I will try to forget that you ever have said it."

And her efforts to forget were seemingly crowned with success. She went to London with him, did faithfully his every behest, worked untiringly at the necessary preparations for their journey and their presumably lengthened sojourn on the Continent, and all without further remonstrance of any kind. At the same time, however, she managed to escape paying or receiving any visits. A few people heard she was in town and came to seek her out, but she contrived to be away or engaged when they called, and to the greater number of her acquaintances her presence in London remained absolutely unknown. Only Margaret Irvine was not so easily put off as the rest, and came again and yet again until she found Muriel at home and, so to speak, in her grasp.

When the friends first met, Margaret began by reproaching Muriel for her want of zeal in not coming to see her. But somehow the reproaches died off her lips. Muriel offered very little excuse for her apparent neglect, but it was plain to Margaret's clear eyes that there was some great and painful reason for it. Some new reason, surely ? since Muriel's loss of fortune and position was an old story now, and had hitherto created no breach in their close friendship. Indeed, what possible difference should it make to either of the two ? But now there was a new reserve about Muriel which Margaret could neither explain nor ignore.

She was so disappointingly reticent about her plans, that Margaret was constrained to discourse of her own instead. She was very busy just then, she told her friend : she had let her beloved little house for a year, and was going to take up her abode with Wentworth. "I don't like it a bit," she protested. "You know how I clung with a thorough old maid's fondness to all my poor little trumpery things : I hate to think of their being handled by strangers, and I shall yearn after them sadly many a time, I know, in Paul's big handsome house. I do like my own chimney corner, Muriel. Nieces are sometimes an infliction as well as a joy to maiden aunts, I assure you!"

"Are you going to take charge of Mabel, then?" Muriel asked.

"Yes. She is rather headstrong, and Paul fancies she will be the better for having an older woman always with her. I wish a little sometimes that I were not that older woman just ready to his hand; or that he would listen to the idea of a companion-chaperone for her, or get her married, or marry himself!" Margaret said, with mock wrath. "However, I have only promised to go for a year; I have not pledged myself for longer. One cannot tell what may happen in a year. Mab might get married, as I say; I am sure I wish she would!"

"It would be a pity—for her father, would it not?" Muriel ventured to say, hating herself for her weakness in putting the question all the while.

"I don't know," Margaret replied, dropping her lighter manner all at once. "She is the light of his eyes; and yet I am always in dread lest she should do something to hurt him. In short, Muriel, Mabel is not another Stella by any means. I find it hard to believe sometimes that she is as near akin to me as Stella was. Happily she is young yet; there is time for her to out-grow her hardness. For she is rather hard, I am afraid."

Had Mabel failed him too? Muriel's heart was so full that she dared not try to speak; and soon afterwards Margaret rose to go.

"If you are really leaving on Thursday," she said, "I suppose there is no use, dear, in asking you to come and see me. But you will write to me as soon as you can, won't you? Where do you think your first halting-place will be?"

"I do not quite know," Muriel answered. She was white with the effort necessary to make her last sacrifice—a sacrifice which she had decided, since her own weakness had been so clearly proved to her, it was her unmistakable duty to make. "And as regards writing, Margaret— will you believe that it is from no want of affec-tion, no want of interest in you, my best, dearest friend, if I do not write? Even if I never do? For I think—I think I had better not."

"Better not write to me?" Margaret repeated in amazement. She could hardly believe that she had heard Muriel aright.

"You see," Muriel said, holding both her friend's hands, and gazing into her face with eyes full of grievous longing and of a yet more bitter anguish of farewell, "I have to take a new departure from henceforward. My life will lie outside England now; it will be better for me not to recur to old things and old friends. It might make me discontented, and anxious to hear about—about things at home, instead of giving myself up to making a new home elsewhere. It will be best for me and for—for them that we should break with each other quite finally, as far as this world is concerned, I think. When I cannot hear anything at all—then perhaps it will be easier. At least, I shall be doing my best."

"I think you have always done that," said Margaret, as well as she could for tears.

Muriel still held her fast. "You are not angry, Margaret? Cannot you see how it is?"

"My dear, how could I be angry with you? But I think you have grown fanciful and nervous and over-scrupulous. Perhaps you are tired, and that has upset your judgment for the moment a little. For I do think that to cut yourself off from all communication with your friends at home is a piece of unnecessary cruelty to yourself and to them."

"It is not unnecessary," Muriel answered, with increasing agitation. "You don't know what a weak, miserable creature I am. I thought, too, that I was strong; I thought so till quite lately. But I am not, I am not! I get so—so easily distracted and impatient; but if I knew that I could never hear from those I had left, that never again as long as I lived could I know anything or ask a single question, perhaps I might do better. And I want so much to do better, Margaret, even if it be ever so difficult—— "

Margaret was shaken out of all her accustomed calm. "It seems so terrible!" she exclaimed. "Why go so far as to make it a resolution? When you are away, you will sometimes find a foreign country lonely, and you will long to write and hear of those who love and care for you, dear child."

As a rule, Margaret Irvine's was a gentle and pleasant voice only; it lacked any finer qualities. But now the depth of the feeling which moved her gave it a passing intonation of Wentworth's, and the very words she uttered brought back other words of Wentworth's own speaking. "I can love and care for you, at least," Muriel seemed to hear him say again with that wonderful tenderness she had found it so hard to resist; and the terrible sweetness of the recollection warned her to stand firm in her resolve.

" I know that well," she answered bravely, but with a sharp throb of inward pain, as she realized even in anticipation how great the bitterness of the unstilled longing would surely be, " and that is the very reason I—I dare not write."

Margaret's face changed. Something of the vague terror that had possessed her in her interview with Muriel after Stella's death returned upon her. She could only clasp the slight figure very tenderly in her arms. " This resolution of yours is a very sad one for me," she said at length. " And yet I will not try to persuade you to rescind it, Muriel. Only you know I love you ; and when happier times come, as I believe and trust they will, you will write to me *then ?* "

And Muriel could not refuse that poor promise to her friend. But for herself she cherished no illusion. Their separation was final : what happier times could be in store for her now ?

CHAPTER XIII.

THE AFTERMATH.

"All things grow sadder to me, one by one."
                                        E. B. BROWNING.

THE twelve months that passed after the Arlinghams left England were eventful months in the
annals of the country. Wales, after a period of
treacherous tranquillity, which deceived all but
the initiated, who knew what fierce and irrecon-
cilable elements of sedition were at work under
the surface calm that seemed to have settled
down upon the Principality, had broken out in
fiercer turbulence than before, and there had not
been wanting many men scattered up and down
the land—men who, as a rule, were neither cowards
nor alarmists—to proclaim that the ominous word
Rebellion would soon have to be substituted for
the less alarming *Riots* at the head of those
columns upon columns of disquieting or startling

telegrams which appeared with depressing regularity in the daily newspapers. However hopefully regarded, the time and the situation were allowed on all hands to be serious, most serious. Wales seemed determined to follow the example of the sister island in extorting virtual autonomy from the imperial authority, and with the sisterly help afforded her, appeared for a brief moment almost strong enough to dictate her own terms. Such were the straits of the Executive, hemmed in between growing disorder and contempt of law on the one hand, and a half-hearted House of Commons on the other, that for a few days only two alternatives of action seemed left open to them: either to concede whatever they demanded to the rebels, or to declare something like a civil war.

Fortunately they refused to adopt the first of these desperate measures, and the necessity for adopting the latter was averted by the Government's holding firmly on its way in repressing violence and disorder, while at the same time promising instant consideration of all reasonable grievances. The Prime Minister and the Secretary for Wales had alike made up their minds that, of the two terrible alternatives presented to them, the second was to be preferred, since

even civil discord would surely prove less deadly
in its effects on all true national life than a base
surrender of the honour and unity of Great
Britain into the hands of men whom Wentworth,
for all his staunch Liberalism, was not ashamed
or afraid to characterize as traitors. These two
Ministers, with Lord Ellesthorpe and Mr. Orme,
made an uncompromising stand for "No con-
cession to rebels," and they managed to drag
timid or recalcitrant members of the Government
along with them in their decision. And soon it
became so clearly apparent that England as a
whole was stoutly on the side of the uncompromising four, that their hesitating colleagues
took courage and became more whole-hearted
in their support of the needful repressive
measures.

It was a stirring year, and for no man more
than for him who presided over the Welsh Office.
Wentworth came and went between Whitehall
and the Principality, and hardly knew himself
which portion of his life was really most harassing and unrestful—whether the days when he
went about Wales with a couple of detectives at
his heels, more than half expecting the sharp
report of a revolver at the corner of every street
and the sharp advent of the tiny bullet which

would end all harassing perplexity and unrest for ever, or the nights when he took his place on the Treasury Bench to meet the never-failing storm of question, calumny, and insult. On the whole, the latter ordeal tried him most, and did far more than any concern for his personal safety to stamp fresh lines on his worn face, and increase the number of grey threads which were beginning to grow noticeably apparent among his thick dark hair. Some of the Welsh "Nationals" were neither particularly refined in mind nor over nice in their choice of language, and they had all heard or read the story of the last election at Coln, unhappily for Wentworth.

But throughout he bore himself manfully, preserving as unwavering a demeanour, night after night, in the face of malignant taunts which cut him to the quick of his sensitive spirit, as he had done at the supreme moment when a furious mob invaded the station at Gwyll-y-Cefn and surrounded the compartment in which he sat, howling madly for his life. This quiet, unshaken courage—which had something pathetic in its steadfastness—won its victory at last over the prejudices even of those stern moralists who for a long time refused utterly to the man the admiration they could not deny to the administrator. For touching Wentworth's administrative powers there could be but one opinion. Before six months were over his strong hand and will were making themselves felt throughout the length and breadth of the disturbed districts; outbreaks were every week becoming fewer in number, and such as did occur were decreasing in violence; order was returning, trade reviving, and England and Scotland alike drew a long breath of relief as the bugbear of the "Welsh scare" began to fade and dwindle into remoter distance.

But there had been terrible moments in those six months: days and nights when the telegraph offices were literally besieged, and the newspaper boys paraded the streets even after midnight; days when calm Philip Irvine went about his work in a fever of anxiety, when Margaret lived so to speak on the rack, and even cold-hearted Mabel Wentworth woke from her self-absorption to share the general terror for the fate of him who walked literally so often with the shadow of death upon him. Margaret never forgot the sudden radiance of her brother's face when she told him long afterwards of one special evening on which Mabel utterly refused to go to some ball, to which she had long been eagerly looking forward, and had remained sitting up all night with her hand locked in Margaret's, till in the grey dawn came the knock of the telegraph boy, bringing the laconic message, "*All quiet here now. Home this evening.*" So intense was the gladness it expressed, that Margaret took courage, feeling that all joy in life was not yet over for Paul.

This especial joy was, however, short-lived. With the cessation of personal danger to her father, came also the cessation of Mabel's temporarily revived interest in him. Perhaps a certain amount of remorse had mingled with that interest, and intensified it; it may be that the idea of Wentworth's being exposed to a sudden violent death had kindled some feeling of regret for past indifference and ingratitude. But once he had escaped this deadly peril and returned to his everyday work in London, the remorse faded away. Wentworth, however, who did not forget so quickly, cherished faithfully the remembrance of Mabel's past concern for his safety, and held the recollection tenderly in his sad heart for many and many a day.

The twelve months of the "Welsh crisis" were fairly at an end, and British home affairs were slowly beginning to resume their normal con-

dition, when Wentworth appeared late one afternoon at his sister's. Margaret had, at the end
of the year agreed upon, returned nominally to
her own abode, though she rarely remained in it
for more than two or three days together, Wentworth's frequent absences from home necessita-
ting her being still often an inmate of his house.

"It is the old story," he said, with that shadow
of a smile which had become habitual to him of
late years; "I want you to come over and take
pity on Mab, as usual."

"Where are you going?" Margaret asked
quickly. "Not to Wales again?" She could
not get over a certain nervous horror of his going
to Wales, though he had frequently assured her
that there was no longer the smallest danger in
his doing so.

"No, not to Wales at present, I am glad to
say. I am going down to Ellesthorpe's from
Saturday to Monday to meet the Premier."

"In preparation for the next Cabinet Council?
Paul, do tell me! You know I am trustworthy,
and I cannot help hearing things whispered. Is
it true what I hear?"

"That I am to have a seat in the Cabinet?
Quite true. It is no secret now; I got the letter
this morning."

Margaret's eyes sparkled. "Ah! I thought it must come soon. Dear Paul, I am so glad!"

"It is pleasant," he said quietly, but rather sadly too, " to find some one who is glad of one's successes. For I suppose this would be called a success."

Then Margaret knew instinctively that he had already told Mabel, and that Mabel had not exerted herself to be at all glad. Probably she had been too preoccupied deciding whether she would have the ivory fan a naval admirer of hers had brought her from China mounted in lace or in feathers for Lady Beatrice Orme's next dance. Margaret thought she might almost be forgiven for hating Mabel a little at that moment.

"Don't go just yet," she entreated, as her brother took up his hat to depart. " I should so like to talk to a rational person for a few minutes, and try and recover my mental balance a little. I have had Lady Clavering here all the morning, and she has nearly chattered away all the mind I have. And I see so little of you nowadays, Paul."

"I have so little leisure, my dear," Paul answered. He was evidently pleased, almost touched, by her anxiety to keep him. "I have two or three notes to write now, but if I may write them here, I can stay a few minutes and talk to you meanwhile. Ordinary sized note-paper, please "—as Margaret promptly unlocked her envelope-case.

He sat down to the pretty writing-table to dash off his letters, and Margaret took a seat opposite, and watched him with sisterly pride. What a noble head he had, and what power and vivacity and resolution there was in the dark face bent over the blotting-book! Only his hair was getting rather grey ; she did not care to see that.

Wentworth looked up and interrupted her silent reflections on the subject of his personal appearance. "Whom did you say you had had with you this morning ? " he inquired.

"Lady Clavering. I think you must know her—a funny little woman with a wonderful tongue. Sir John Clavering has a very pretty place in Holmshire, called Newhaye. I went down there once for a week, and was nearly talked to death."

"Holmshire ? " Wentworth drew his dark brows together for a moment. Then he looked down again and went on writing rapidly. "Talk-ing of Holmshire," he said, "have you any news lately of your Holmshire friend, Mrs. Arlingham? "

"How strange!" Margaret exclaimed. "Lady Clavering has just been asking me the same question; in fact, she called here on purpose to ask it. And I could only tell her that I had no news at all."

"I thought Lady Clavering herself was a great personal friend of Mrs. Arlingham's," Wentworth observed.

"She has known Muriel all her life. I had half a hope—as I told her—when I saw her arrive, that she might have brought me some news, instead of coming to ask for it. But it appears that Muriel has not written to the Claverings either. It is very curious and very sad."

"When did she last write to you?" Wentworth inquired, still without lifting his eyes from the paper.

"She has never written to me at all," Margaret answered sorrowfully.

Wentworth looked up at this. "Do you mean that you have never heard from her since she left England more than a year ago?" he demanded, with a kind of stern surprise, laying down his pen.

"Never. And I have no reason to feel astonished at her silence, for she told me when we parted that she should not write, either to me or to any of her friends in England. But I never dreamed that she would have kept her word so inflexibly."

"Ah!" Wentworth drew in his breath so sharply that it sounded as if he uttered an exclamation. "That is a curious whim of your friend's, to cut herself off from every one. She has relatives living in Holmshire, hasn't she?" He had taken up his pen again, and was busily addressing several envelopes.

"Her relations are all out in India now, except her father. And he has recently married an American lady, and gone over to spend some months in his new wife's country. Had he been at home, Lady Clavering would of course have gone to him for news, instead of coming to me."

"Then you do not even know where your friends are at present?" Wentworth was now beginning to fold his correspondence.

"I am not sure; I heard where they were a little while back. But speak in the singular number, please. Mr. Arlingham is no friend of mine. His wife is entirely thrown away upon him, except in so far as the trial of being his wife has served to bring out the intrinsic beauty of her character. Why she ever married him, or how she could ever have persuaded herself that she was in love with him at any time, I cannot understand."

Wentworth frowned. "Women marry for many reasons," he said shortly.

"Many women do, certainly; but Muriel Arlingham is unlike and above most women."

"These things seem to go by a law of contrasts," Wentworth returned. "And the pity of it is, that the noblest women so often do marry the most contemptible men."

"A commonplace admirable man would not have satisfied me as Muriel's husband," Margaret said; "but in Mr. Arlingham there was absolutely nothing to admire whatever. He was utterly unworthy of her in every way. Don't you think so?"

Wentworth was stooping forward to stamp his letters. "I never yet met," he answered in a quiet voice—through which, nevertheless, there ran a thrill of intense passion—"the man whom I should have judged worthy of her. But for her husband to remain what Arlingham remained, showed a lowness of nature beyond all remedy. If the man had had the very smallest grain of nobleness in him, it would have come out at her touch. He would have grown better simply by being near her."

Margaret did not answer. A formless suspicion that had long haunted her mind began to take colour and shape there; she fancied she could guess now why Paul had never married again.

" You have heard *of* your friend, though not from her, I think you said ? " Wentworth re-marked, after a few seconds' pause. He had risen from his chair, and was putting his little heap of notes together.

" I heard of her two months ago from the Dalrymples. She was then at Venice, and they met her by chance in St. Mark's one day."

" I hope she was well ? "

" Mrs. Dalrymple said she looked very white and delicate, though not precisely ill. But they did not talk much; she was shy and nervous, and evidently shrank from conversation. They proposed calling on her, but she made so many difficulties that they felt it was best not to press it."

" What did Mrs. Dalrymple say besides ? " Wentworth inquired, coming nearer to Mar-garet, and standing over her as he put his question. She could not refuse to answer it, though she trembled at the turn the conver-sation was taking.

" Very little about Mrs. Arlingham herself.

I fancy their interview with her was of the briefest. The rest was only hearsay—the gossip of the English colony at Venice, which one must of course accept with due reservation. A great deal of what Mrs. Dalrymple heard may have been untrue, or, at least, a gross exaggeration of the truth. I hope so, at least, with all my heart!"

"I suppose," said Wentworth, setting his teeth and looking his sister straight in the face—"I suppose it is said that—that her husband ill-treats her?"

Margaret could not answer for a moment; the look in her brother's eyes terrified her too much. "Not that positively," she said hurriedly, when she had recovered herself. "When he is —well, quite himself—I fancy he is only indifferent and neglectful; but since he lost his money and allowed himself to be drawn into associating with people beneath him, he is not always himself by any means; and then—— Oh, my poor Muriel! What a fate for such a woman as she is!"

Compassion for her friend had overpowered every other consideration in Margaret's mind for the moment.

Wentworth made no reply. He dared not,

lest he should betray himself, and one whom he thought of far more than himself.

"It is one of those cases of hopeless misery which rouse a feeling of blind rebellion in one at times," Margaret said—most injudiciously, it must be acknowledged. "Why does she not leave him? I do not believe any law, human or Divine, could be invoked to compel her to stay."

"She will never leave him," Wentworth answered, forgetting his part. "She will work out that penance to the end."

Margaret glanced uneasily at his stern, pale face, and judged it well that he should know the whole scope of Muriel's parting resolve. "When I knew where the poor child was, and how things were with her, I could hardly forbear sending her a few lines," she said. "Even if she did not choose to answer my letter, I fancied a little affection might do her good. But on reflection I dared not, remembering how earnest she seemed in wishing to hear from no one."

"Why does she wish not to hear?" Wentworth asked.

"Because," said Margaret, who could barely restrain her tears, "she wished to forget all about England and those in it. I can only follow out her wish, though I cannot understand it."

"Cannot you?" replied Wentworth, with a touch of scorn. "I think I can. But I must be going now. Good-bye. I—I am sorry to hear what you have just told me."

Margaret had spoken of "a feeling of blind rebellion," but her wildest fears could never have pictured to her such a storm as she had conjured up in her half-brother's breast. Why had he yielded to his paltry scruples—or, rather, to his unmanly love of self and fair fame—when Muriel's fate had been in his hands a year before? It was he who had drawn back, not she. At that moment it would scarcely have needed more than a word and a touch—he had known it well at the time—to make her his, safe for ever from all the ghastly possibilities of her present wretched existence. And her misery was due in the main to him—to Wentworth himself! Had he not wrecked her youth, she would never have become Arlingham's wife; and then, when the opportunity had been given him of rescuing her from the worst consequences of that fatal marriage, he had flung it aside. She might have been saved, had he so pleased.

Saved? Nay, the very word itself rebuked him. Saved, indeed, from a life of fear and anxiety and undeserved suffering, the very thought of which wrung his heart; but how? By exchanging it for one of self-reproach and shame and lifelong remorse—the only life possible to such a woman as Muriel had she been induced in a moment of madness to leave the strait, hard path of duty and obedience. Wentworth, expiating even at this hour his own past sin in the knowledge of her suffering, knew in his heart that she was happier than he. No cloud rested on her soul now as she looked up to God or out upon the world; there would be none resting there when she came to die.

I think there was something like an inarticulate prayer in Wentworth's mind that Muriel's might not be a very long life.

He had been walking homewards all the while that these thoughts surged and struggled in turn for the mastery within him, and by the time he reached his own house he was growing calmer. He must write to the Premier now, and then he would have to go down to the Welsh Office for an hour; but there was no hurry, for he could go on straight to the House from Whitehall. No; on second thoughts he must return home again, for he had left a message for Mabel that she might expect him at dinner, and she might be disappointed if he failed her. The thought of her possible disappointment would not allow him to make the excuse he longed to make, and so escape from the gay talk and the laughter and the bright scenes which must always surround Mabel. Ah, well! he had had long practice now in the art of smiling on serenely in spite of a broken heart and a spirit wounded to the death; and, let his own suffering be what it might, not a shadow of it must be permitted to fall on her, his light-hearted darling!

He could hear her clear voice and rippling laugh issuing from her own special sitting-room upstairs, the door of which stood ajar. She was busy consulting with her faithful maid and quondam nurse over a new dress she was to wear that night, and a rustle of silken draperies mingled itself with her words every now and then. Wentworth paused for an instant at the door on his way upstairs, and even laid his hand upon it, but he did not go in. A note lying on a little table in the lobby caught his eye, and he turned aside to open it.

It was only a note of congratulation from one

of his colleagues, and he was putting it down half read, when he heard his daughter say, " Mr. Wentworth is going to dine at the House, I suppose, Dickinson ? " Mabel affected a formal style in speaking of her father to strangers and dependants.

" No, Miss Mabel," replied Dickinson's voice. " He told me to say he would be home to dinner at eight, and asked if your new dress had come in good time."

" Dear me, what a nuisance ! " Mabel exclaimed pettishly. " He will be expecting me to dress before dinner, that he may be able to see how I look, and I really can't do that. I should be sure to crush all this tulle most terribly, and spoil the whole effect."

" No need to do that, Miss Mabel. Mr. Wentworth said he meant to go with you to Lady Hatherop's this evening for an hour or two. I was to tell you to let Mrs. St. John know she need not call for you, and say you would join her at the ball."

" How tiresome ! " Mabel's clear level voice rang out remorselessly ; every syllable it uttered was cruelly distinct. " What on earth put that into father's head, I wonder ? I hate going to dances with him ; I would ten times sooner have gone with Mrs. St. John ! "

228 THE REPENTANCE OF PAUL WENTWORTH.

A few minutes before, Wentworth had imagined that he knew what the extreme of suffering meant, and that there was nothing further for him to experience in the matter of pain. Now he found he had been mistaken.

He received the blow dealt him unawares very quietly, however. For a moment he put his hand to his breast, as a man who had been struck to the heart might do—perhaps it were not altogether a figure of speech to say that he had just been so struck—and then turned and continued his way upstairs. In about twenty minutes he came down again, and this time he went straight into his daughter's sitting-room. She was tying up a bouquet of Maréchal Niel roses with long streamers of pale yellow ribbon, Dickinson standing by, admiring and assisting.

"Mabel," Wentworth said, in a voice which he tried to make as natural as possible, "have you written to Mrs. St. John to tell her not to call for you this evening?"

Mabel was startled by her father's manner. It was not angry, nor even severe, yet it frightened her vaguely. "I—I was just going to," she answered, putting down her flowers in a hurry.

"Don't disturb yourself," Wentworth rejoined, with the faintest touch of irony in his tone.

"You need not write at all now—indeed, I am glad you have not written—for I am not going to Lady Hatherop's after all."

"Are you not? What a pity!" Mabel responded. The words smote Wentworth with a double pang; their careless politeness was so like Alice! He wondered, too, what Dickinson's opinion of Mabel's sincerity might be.

"But you are coming home to dinner, at least, father?" the girl continued.

Half an hour earlier that question would have thrilled Wentworth with unreasonable delight. Now he only answered, rather sternly, "No; I shall not do that either. I shall dine at the House, probably."

Again Mabel felt vaguely uneasy. "I wish you could have seen me in my new gown; it is just perfection," she said with facile hypocrisy. "Look, is not the colour lovely?"

Wentworth glanced at the much-belauded *confection* as it lay on the sofa. "It is a very pretty dress," he answered. "I dare say it will suit you very well." Then he made his final effort. He took Mabel in his arms, and kissed her. "Good-bye, dear. I hope you will enjoy yourself this evening," he said very gently.

Half touched, half anxious to conciliate him

for she knew not what reason, Mabel responded with a clinging caress. But at that Wentworth put her from him quickly. "Don't!" he said sharply. "You hurt me." And with those enigmatical words he went away.

At the House only smiles and congratulations awaited him; at the clubs men gathered in knots and talked of his new dignity and of how well he had earned it, of his year of great work for the nation, and of the honours that surely awaited him in the future. For his past—he had lived it down, men said, or was living it down; and, besides, who would remember to set bygone frailties against the solid achievements of one who had deserved so well of his country? He was fairly on the road to a magnificent success in public life; he was overleaping every obstacle in his onward march to political power and influence, just as he had done once before in his legal career. Lucky? Was there ever such a lucky fellow! Everywhere on the crest of the wave—his very defeats turned into victories.

There is a success which knoweth its own bitterness, as there is a defeat in which dwells a hidden joy. There may have been a cruel canker gnawing at the root of that very bay tree which to David seemed to flourish in insolent

pride; and even in these latter days the poet's
assertion—

ƪ "Denn alle Schuld rächt sich auf Erden,"

is more generally and literally true than we
think for. Only, men wear such cunningly
devised masks now, that the majority of on-
lookers are deceived; and it would have been
hard to convince those who met Paul Wentworth that night—those who heard his ready
answer in debate, received his easily turned
reply to their congratulatory speeches, and
marked his self-contained bearing as he sat on
the Treasury Bench—that this same brilliant,
fortunate man, this Polykrates of the hour, was
all the while crying out silently in the recesses
of his tortured soul, " My punishment is greater
than I can bear."

CHAPTER XIV.

HELEN'S DIPLOMACY.

"The not so very false, as falsehood goes—
  The spinning out and drawing fine, you know ;
  Really novel-writing, of a sort,
  Acting, improvising, make-believe—
  Surely not downright cheatery ! "

R. BROWNING.

ON a beautiful day early in the following May,
Muriel was sitting on a balcony of the great
hotel at Cadenabbia, looking out on what is
perhaps the loveliest prospect in all the lovely
Italian lakeland. It was late in the afternoon.
A pleasant breeze, just strong enough to temper
the fervour of the sun's rays, and to set the
numerous fleet of light boats which dotted the
steel-coloured waters of the lake in every direction dancing and rocking gaily, was ruffling all
that beautiful expanse of water which reaches
from the Balbianello Point to where Menaggio

nestles under the great wooded mountains dividing Como from her sister lake of Lugano. Beyond the promontory where white Bellagio lay literally ablaze with fiery golden sunshine, the wind was blowing in greater earnest. It came sweeping up the Lecco arm of the lake in strong warm gusts which crested the waves it created with foam, and tossed a great flat boat, laden with grain (and on its way down from Gravedona, no doubt), so remorselessly from side to side that the swarthy red-capped sailors who manned it were obliged to lower their square brown sails and take to their huge oars instead. They did not seem affected by this misfortune, however, and toiled on patiently and cheerily, three men labouring doggedly at each oar in their curious native fashion of standing upright and pulling forward, and breaking now and then into a snatch of song by the way. Opposite Menaggio and away to the left, where the waves seemed roughest and highest, Varenna—most picturesque of all lake-side villages—lay half in shadow, clustering round its tall campanile; and in a cleft of the hills close by Muriel could descry a perpetually recurring flash of snowy whiteness— sole visible sign of the half-concealed cascade which, on nearer approach, reveals itself as the

Fiume Latte, a true "river of milk." Though the snow still lay on the Val Tellina range, and the season was nominally that of spring, Cadenabbia already rejoiced in the full glory of summer warmth and beauty; everywhere was the scent of roses, and the rhododendrons and azaleas in the gardens of the Villa Carlotta clothed the slopes on which they grew with an unbroken sheet of bloom down to the very water's edge. Muriel sat on her balcony with a look of quiet satisfaction on her face, drinking in the loveliness that surrounded her with every breath she drew, and listening to the sweet deep-toned bells of San Giovanni sounding solemnly across the water.

Hour after hour went by, and she still sat there in tranquil solitude, seemingly well contented. Helen Bretherton, now her constant companion, had an adventurous spirit, and liked to do and see all that came in her way to be done and seen; so Muriel, whose energy had forsaken her of late, was perforce becoming used to spend much of her time alone. Perhaps this frequent solitude had charms for her; which was a fortunate circumstance, since, except for her enterprising cousin, she was alone in the world altogether.

It was little more than a year before this special May afternoon that Miss Bretherton, coming in late one evening from a college concert at Oxford, had been startled to find this telegram lying on her hall table :—

"*From the* REV. EDWARD BRIND,
    "*British Chaplain at Venice,*
    "*To* MISS HELEN BRETHERTON,
    "*25, Ridley Gardens, Oxford.*

"*Mr. Geoffrey Arlingham died this morning, after a week's illness. Come instantly to Mrs. Arlingham.*"

And Helen had gone as she was asked, scarcely able to credit the tidings conveyed to her; but she found them literally true. Jack had "got a chill"—one of those mysterious and deadly chills which seem peculiar to Italy beyond all other countries and climates—and it had made short work of a constitution never strong, and enfeebled for some time past by constant over-fatigue, excitement, and self-indulgence. He had died almost without a struggle to retain his hold on a life of which he had grown more than half weary, and bitterly conscious of "having made a hopeless mess of everything," as he said regretfully—thus pathetically recurring in his last hours to his old boyish expression of self-dissatisfaction.

In that concluding scene of his life history he had turned wistfully to his wife, and Muriel had not failed him. She had always been so ready to pardon his wrongs towards herself at all times that he knew he had hardly to ask her forgiveness before it would be granted him; but he wanted more of her than her forgiveness—he needed her to soothe, uphold, and encourage. And all these things Muriel did, and did alone and un-assisted. While her husband lived, no one, she was determined, should come on the plea of assisting her, his wife, to disturb his dying hours by their stranger presence, or to witness the bitterness of his unavailing regrets. Only when she had actually closed his eyes in that sleep that knows no waking, would she yield to any suggestions to send for friend or relative. Then she said, "Send for Helen—my cousin. And tell her to come *soon*."

Muriel was very ill herself after this. Ill, not of any definite complaint on which a physician could have put his finger, but with that utter prostration of mind and body which so often follows a long period of unnatural tension suddenly terminated by a great shock. Vague and intangible as her malady was, she was nevertheless very near dying of it. But youth and the accumulated strength of twenty-seven years of unbroken health triumphed, and she struggled slowly back to life again.

Perhaps, after all, her illness was a blessing to her. In that long-enforced inaction and utter seclusion from the world, and in the inevitable absorption of her thoughts to a great extent in bodily ills and discomforts, her overstrained mind had its opportunity of lying torpid, becoming gradually relaxed, and then slowly waking up, with the return of physical well-being, to a new set of feelings and impressions. The painful past was indeed still very present with her, but her vivid recollection of it had been mercifully dulled by those protracted months of suffering weakness, when it had so often seemed doubtful whether she herself might not slip away from life for sheer want of will and strength to live. Now that she was better, she knew well that she had never really wished to die; she had merely experienced for a brief space that sense of excessive exhaustion which makes life itself seem a thing of too much effort to be endured. Her youth was full of bitter memories—of peril and conflict and grievous disappointment; but life was in itself good, and returning health delicious, and she was yet young enough to hope that the future might hold better things in store for her than the past had done. She defined nothing, planned nothing, expected nothing; only this vague confidence was upon her, gradually filling her darkened world with sunshine.

Her thoughts of her husband had become infinitely kind and pitying thoughts. Now that it was a sacred duty to think of him as tenderly and as reverently as possible, she felt it no sin to try and forget as far as possible the dark years of their married life, and to revert in her recollections rather to those earlier days when Jack was her playmate, her friend, and finally her proud and happy accepted lover. The Jack of her girlhood seemed to have little in common with the moody, dissipated man whom she had vainly sought to soften and restrain by un-murmuring patience and a life of uncomplaining devotion which he failed to recognize till he lay on his deathbed; but it made her at once happier and more sorrowful to think of him in his boyish simplicity. For the Jack of those days her tears flowed indeed, but with less bitterness. She was glad to remember that a touch of his old simple self had returned to him at the last: it made the memory of their final parting less terrible.

When months had passed away, when the first shock of her husband's almost sudden death was over and she was at length well enough to think about herself at all, she found that her chief sensation was one of restfulness, of cessation from struggle of any kind, and of an almost absolute passivity of feeling as regarded the future. All wish to try and order her life in any way had gone out of her. She had made so deadly a mistake in trying to order it for herself once, that she had conceived a kind of dread not only of any action which should partake of the nature of an effort after happiness, but of any decision which could seriously affect her future at all. She preferred sitting still with folded hands to see what that future might bring her. Even in all minor matters she let Helen Bretherton decide for her, gladly accepting her cousin's choice rather than incur the responsibility of choosing for herself.

Thus, when the autumn came, and she was strong enough to leave Venice, and Helen proposed a winter and spring in Italy as safer than returning to England just then, she acquiesced unresistingly. Happily, means were not wanting to her to carry out the plan. Eversleigh, indeed, had passed into the possession of a distant heir, and the poor remnants of Jack's fortune barely sufficed to satisfy his creditors, but by the death of her godmother, which took place about a month after that of her husband, Muriel had inherited such an income as would henceforward be amply sufficient for her simple wants, and that without undue economy. The helpless anxiety concerning material provision for the future and the ever-increasing pressure of debt were among the heavy weights lifted at last from her slight shoulders. No marvel that such relief induced a peaceful frame of mind to which she had long been a stranger.

This sense of peace deepened as the winter went by. Little by little, the feeling of absolute freedom from any necessity for conflict grew upon her, filling all her mind with a calm which in itself was rapture to one so storm-tossed as she had been for years. Gradually, too, the memory which for years she had been resolutely crushing, the love which had hitherto been only her sharpest misery and her chief source of self-reproach, reasserted itself—shyly at first, for it was long before she dared allow herself to dwell upon it, or could cease to regard it as a dangerous weakness. But when once she had summoned courage to look it full in the face—when she had recognized that it was mere self-deception to ignore its existence, and a piece of unworthy and childish sentimentalism to persuade herself that pitying sorrow for Jack's wasted life and pathetic death had annihilated the one master passion of her heart, a great and quiet content fell upon her. She might think freely of Paul Wentworth now, and for the present she asked no more than this. To be able to dwell proudly, yet without incurring self-condemnation, on his growing fame and increasing honour among men; to read every recorded word that fell from his lips with eager, blameless eyes; above all, to have leave to hold the recollection of him in her solitary heart and to utter his name tenderly in her prayers—all this was enough and more than enough for one who had been so long forbidden to love him, and who found in the simple luxury of loving a continual source of passionate delight. I do not think Muriel questioned much whether Wentworth, for his part, still loved her. Perhaps she took that for granted, deeming it impossible that his love could be less steadfast than her own.

Neither was she, as yet, very anxious to see him. For a long time she could not well have endured the thought of such a meeting; and afterwards she was well content to wait for it, having a happy confidence that in fitting time it would surely take place. When Wentworth thought it right and well to seek her, he would do so: she did not even trouble herself to conjecture how soon that day would arrive.

Of him, except indirectly, she heard nothing. Margaret, when she had learned Muriel's widowhood, had indeed ventured to write, and when Muriel's long illness came to an end, she had answered her friend's letter, a response which finally led to the resumption of their old correspondence—but in her now frequent and regular epistles Margaret scrupulously avoided all mention of her half-brother. She spoke often of Philip, and occasionally of Mabel; but touching Mabel's father she said nothing at all. Muriel, wearying sometimes in spite of her new-found content for one little mention of the beloved name, began to think that the interdict she had laid formerly on Margaret's letters had scarcely been a needful one.

When it was time to leave her quiet winter retreat at San Remo, and she found herself actually on the road to England, this repressed desire for tidings of some kind grew stronger. Perhaps the season itself stirred all the latent youth and hope within her; perhaps the very loveliness of the scenes through which she was passing—for, at Miss Bretherton's suggestion, they were travelling slowly homewards by way of the Italian lakes—rekindled the old natural longing for some positive beauty and happiness to illumine her still, shadowy life, and render it more in harmony with its surroundings; perhaps the very knowledge that she was drawing week by week nearer to London, and therefore to Wentworth, combined with all the rest to disturb the dreamy peace in which she had dwelt so long with presentiments and anticipations and half-acknowledged hopes which set her heart beating at every "sunset touch" of remembrance, and brought such new light into her eyes and colour to her cheeks that Miss Bretherton decided she was regaining all the bloom and beauty of her girlhood. Helen wondered at the change, and cast about in search of a reason for it, but could find none.

She had been speculating on the subject while climbing the Sasso San Martino, and came in from her excursion with her mind still full of

the unsolved problem. She went straight to
Muriel on the balcony, for she had met the waiter
on the stairs bringing up the afternoon letters,
and he had given her three for Mrs. Arlingham.

The first, which was from Margaret Irvine,
Muriel opened eagerly ; and having read it, she
put it aside with a heightened colour and a shy,
half-suppressed smile. But she did not speak of
the contents. When she had glanced through
the remainder of her correspondence, however,
she turned to her cousin, saying, " Marjory hopes
to arrive this evening, but she does not say
whether by way of Lugano or Varese."

Marjory St. John was the daughter of an
invalid retired judge who wintered regularly at
San Remo. Mrs. Arlingham had made a kind of
pet of the girl during the past winter, and had
invited her to join her at the lakes for a week
or two before she returned to England.

" Very like Marjory, to be so vague in her
announcements," responded Helen Bretherton,
who was rather jealous of the young lady in
question. " Have you heard from your step-
mother too ? "

" No, this letter is from Mr. Earle—my cousin-
in-law, Fred Earle. He is coming to Cadenabbia," Muriel said, with a peculiar little smile,

gazing at the steamer which was slowly but steadily making its way over from Bellagio, "and he writes to know which hotel we are staying at, as he doesn't want to be a long way off from us. Poor Fred! his ideas of Cadenabbia are rather magnificently extensive, I am afraid."

Helen Bretherton had found the key to her problem at last! She knew perfectly now what it was that had wrought so great a change in Muriel during the last few weeks. How blind she had been not to see sooner what the young man's constant comings and goings at San Remo meant! His following them to Cadenabbia was of course conclusive; and such a marriage would soon make up to her dear Muriel for all she had suffered in the past. A bright, frank, clever fellow, rising fast in the diplomatic service too.

Helen was fond of leaping rather hastily to conclusions, you perceive. She had almost settled the details of the wedding, while Muriel was still watching the approaching steamer with that half-smile on her lips, and in her mind going over the postscript of Margaret's letter: "*I am going to take Mabel to the Isle of Wight for three weeks to-morrow. Paul starts to-day for a short holiday in Italy. You will see him, I*

hope." Margaret's significant silence was significantly broken at last.

But although Miss Bretherton was brimming
over with misplaced pleasurable agitation, she
knew Muriel too well to let it appear; and the
impulsive, romantic little woman with the
colourless hair and eyes was clever enough to
dissimulate well on occasion. She took up a
basket from the table, feeling that, tired as she
was, she must do something to work off her
suppressed excitement.

"Our flowers are growing rather faded," she
observed. "I think I will go out and get a few
before dinner."

"My dear Helen," Muriel said, leaning back
in her chair, and squeezing Margaret's precious
letter tenderly between her hands, "you are
quite a prodigy of energy! But I really believe
your energy will kill you one of these days:
you will die of perpetual motion. Do leave
the flowers till to-morrow! They will do very
well."

But Miss Bretherton would not be persuaded.
To-morrow was Sunday; and by to-morrow the
roses would be quite dead. She must really go
and look for something to replace them.

"Very well," Muriel said resignedly. "A

wilful man, you know—still more a wilful
woman. Only if you are really going, please
wait at the landing-stage till the steamer comes
in. If Marjory has elected to come by Lugano
and Porlezza, she will probably be on it, and
you can tell her to come up to me here."

Miss Bretherton assented readily. She did
not much like Marjory St. John, but she liked
being the first to meet her. Muriel, from her
luxurious lounge on the balcony, watched the
trim little figure standing in an attitude of
expectation while the steamer hove to, and
silently extolled her cousin's good nature and
kindness of heart for the thousandth time.

A good many people were disembarking, and
a good many more were lounging about to see
them arrive, so there was something of a crowd
in the neighbourhood of the landing-stage;
and though it is situated almost immediately
opposite that particular balcony on which
Muriel was sitting, she found it difficult to
ascertain whether Marjory St. John was among
the flock of arrivals or no. Apparently no; for
if the girl were there, Helen would not have
lingered to talk to the tall man with whom she
had just shaken hands, and who looked almost
like—— Was it possible? Yes, it was he,

Wentworth himself! He must have travelled as quickly as his sister's letter.

Muriel was on her feet for a moment; then she checked herself, and resolutely sat down again. It could only be a question of minutes now before they met: Helen would bring him up at once. No, Helen had turned aside with him into the plantain avenue which leads to the Villa Carlotta, talking earnestly. What could those two possibly have to say to each other?

It was a pity that Muriel should have been out of earshot of the speakers, one of whom was literally and indeed Paul Wentworth. And a most unwelcome apparition he was in Helen Bretherton's eyes. Unwelcome he would have been at any time, but at the present juncture his appearance on the scene might be little short of disastrous to Helen's newborn hopes and schemes. She had never forgotten the suspicions she had conceived at Oxford two years previously; and, great as was her personal antipathy to Wentworth, in whom she firmly believed no good and all evil things to dwell, she had an exaggerated opinion of his powers of fascination. Her old dislike and distrust of him returned upon her in full force; and though she was not, as a rule, a very brave woman, she determined that she would make one valiant effort before she permitted this man to interpose the memory of his unscrupulous passion between her beloved Muriel and the young lover *sans peur et sans reproche*, who was already on his way to Cadenabbia to woo her.

But to produce the effect she desired she must not let her animosity to Wentworth appear; she must be "diplomatic," as she phrased it. Therefore she assumed a very cordial manner, and greeted Mr. Wentworth with quite a respectable show of effusive pleasure. Where was he staying? When had he left England? Was his daughter with him? How strange that they should meet at the very moment of his landing!

"I left England the day before yesterday," Wentworth said briefly, in answer to the eager string of questions addressed to him, "and I reached Bellagio just an hour ago. I am travelling quite alone. Having heard that you were staying here—you and Mrs. Arlingham—I came over. Is Mrs. Arlingham in?"

He spoke very simply and manfully, without any attempt at conventional subterfuges, and Helen began to think it might be hard to turn him from what was evidently a settled purpose.

"This is very kind of you," she said. "My cousin is at home, certainly, but she is just now resting before dinner." Which statement, as far as it went, was fairly veracious.

"I hope she is not ill?" Wentworth said, anxiously. "I understood from my sister that her illness was quite a thing of the past."

"It is, indeed," Helen replied. "She has recovered her health entirely, I am glad to say. But she is still rather languid at times, and it is late in the day—— "

"I see," interrupted Wentworth, trying to master his impatience; "you think it too late for a visit. It is very late, I suppose. But I was thinking of sleeping at Tremezzo: a friend of mine has a villa there. Perhaps Mrs. Arlingham might be inclined to see me if I called to-morrow? I will come at whatever hour you think best likely to suit her."

Miss Bretherton appeared to hesitate a moment. "I should really be afraid to say," she answered reluctantly at last. "The truth is, Mr. Wentworth, my cousin rather shrinks from seeing visitors. I do not quite know how to propose to her to receive you."

The old dark flush came into Wentworth's cheek. He began to suspect this little woman

with the light eyelashes of being his enemy—
which, indeed she was—and of trying to stand
in his path. " Will you at least ask her on my
behalf ? " he urged, with as much gentleness and
deference of manner as he could force himself to
assume.

" I am sure I would gladly do so—— " Helen
began. Then she checked herself, and said impulsively, " Mr. Wentworth, you are a generous
man ; I am sure I may trust you."

Wentworth bent his head stiffly. He did not
believe that Miss Bretherton really thought him
either generous or trustworthy ; and he was
perfectly right, for she did not. But she believed him to be very proud, which she fancied
might answer her purpose equally well.

" My cousin, as you know, and as all her
friends must know," said the little woman
tremulously, for what she was doing frightened
her dreadfully, " has had a very sad life of late
years. Her marriage was a terrible mistake,
and her husband, poor fellow, made her extremely unhappy. She is only just recovering
from the shock of his death. Following, as it
did, on so much previous trouble and anxiety,
it had a very injurious effect upon her health.
It is my endeavour, my earnest endeavour, that,

as far as possible, she shall have nothing brought before her to remind her of that miserable time." Helen paused, and looked appealingly at Wentworth.

He bent his dark brows in ominous determination. "And therefore you think it is better that Mrs. Arlingham should not see me—is it not so? —for fear of reviving painful memories? I have taken that question into consideration too, Miss Bretherton. For which reason I never had any intention of calling on Mrs. Arlingham until I had received her express permission to do so. If she feels that my presence is likely to cause her the slightest pain, she has only to decline my visit."

Wentworth was speaking now with so much resolution that Helen felt she must go considerably further than she had ventured yet, if she wished to gain her end.

"I only gave you part of my reason just now," she said hurriedly, and it was at this point in the conversation that she took a few steps in the direction of the plantain avenue, having become suddenly alive to the fact that she and her companion were standing in full view of Muriel's balcony. "I will tell you the other part too. Why should not I?" she added in a burst of

confidence. " You have known Mrs. Arlingham
for many years, I believe—almost from her childhood. I may therefore say to you frankly that
I have good hope now of something more than a
mere obliteration of her sorrows for my cousin,
and that she is on the eve of a great happiness
which will, I trust, fully make up to her for all
she has suffered. But her mind has become very
sensitive, and scrupulous, and easily disturbed,
and I dread the effect of anything recalling what
was so painful and distressing in the past. I
dread it inexpressibly, Mr. Wentworth." Helen
was very much agitated and very much in
earnest. There could be no doubt on either of
those points.

" I perfectly understand your motives, Miss
Bretherton," returned Wentworth, who had all
at once grown deadly pale. " They are clear to
me, quite clear. What is not quite so clear to me
as yet is the nature, or rather the full extent, of
the fact at which you have hinted. Am I to
understand that your cousin is about to be
married ? "

Helen Bretherton was apt in the heat of her
various impulses to exaggerate the truth occasionally—she had never yet in her life deliberately
falsified it. But the temptation to save Muriel

with a word was great, and she had gone almost too far to draw back now with honour to herself, while a glance at Wentworth's inflexible countenance convinced her that nothing but a plain downright assertion would have any weight with him. It was only doing a very small evil that great good might come of it; and Fred Earle was actually on his way to Cadenabbia—she would merely be anticipating events by a few days.

"Yes," she answered unflinchingly. "But it is a secret at present." She congratulated herself, as she spoke, on the way in which Mr. Wentworth had framed his question. "About to be married" just fitted the peculiar circumstances under which she felt herself forced to reply with an anticipation of the coming truth.

Half an hour later, when she came up to Muriel with a basketful of azaleas, she found her standing in the sitting-room eagerly awaiting her return, with a strange brilliancy in her eyes and a great spot of feverish colour burning on either delicate cheek. Helen began to expatiate on the beauty of the azaleas, but Muriel could not listen to her raptures long without interrupting them.

"Whom did I see you talking to after the

steamer came in?" she asked with assumed carelessness. " Wasn't it Mr. Wentworth?"

So, in spite of Helen's tardy precautions, Muriel had seen him! "Yes, it was Mr. Wentworth. He had just come over from Bellagio."

" Is he staying here ?"

"No, he has gone on to Tremezzo, I believe. I fancy he is not making a long stay anywhere. Curiously enough, Muriel, he knows Mr. Earle well, and says he is perhaps the most rising man in the diplomatic service."

. "Does he?" rejoined Muriel eagerly. " What did he say about him?" She would have asked the same question just as eagerly had she heard that Paul had been discussing the merits of the man who sold cherries in front of the hotel; but Miss Bretherton smiled, well-pleased at this new proof, as she deemed it, of Muriel's inability to conceal her interest in Fred Earle.

"Nothing very particular; only vague generalities of approbation and admiration," she responded cautiously. "Let me see, what did he say besides? Oh, he talked of his journey a little: he had come straight through from London, he said, and was quite alone. It would look better if he took that poor motherless girl of his about with him a little more, it seems to me."

Muriel did not heed, perhaps did not even hear, this moral reflection of her cousin's. Her mind was otherwise occupied. Tremezzo? It was very near. He might easily walk over to Cadenabbia before breakfast, unless he found it quicker and more convenient to take a boat, or there was an early steamer. Only why had he put off coming even so long as to-morrow?

"Did you ask Mr. Wentworth to come in?" she demanded, going into the balcony to fetch the letters she had left there.

"He seemed to think it was late for a visit," Helen answered evasively.

"Well, it would have been rather late, I suppose," Muriel returned, with that happy smile just parting her lips again. "He would probably have made us late for dinner; as it is, I believe I shall hardly have time to change my dress now. But it does not really matter in the least."

Certainly it did not matter—how could anything in the world matter now? He would come to-morrow; he would surely come to-morrow. All night the carillons sounding over the water sang her that one chime.

CHAPTER XV.

AT ST. STEPHEN'S.

" I never heard but two voices in my life that frightened me
by their sweetness. They made me feel as if there might be
constituted a creature with such a chord in his voice to some
string in another's soul, if he but spoke, she would leave all
and follow him, though it were into the jaws of Erebus."—
O. W. HOLMES.

BUT he did not come on the morrow, nor on the
next day, nor on the day which succeeded that.
Slowly confident anticipation gave way to cruel
suspense, and then, having passed through every
stage of that hope deferred which maketh the
heart sick, ended in a dead calm of despair.
When the third evening closed in without bringing him, Muriel knew that he would never come.

She did not try to deceive herself as to the
reasons which kept him away. Only one could
exist: a desire to avoid meeting her. He knew
she was there—Helen had told him ; Helen had

even invited him to come and see her, and he had pleaded the lateness of the hour as an excuse for declining the invitation. He would not even spend a single night in Cadenabbia, lest he should encounter her by chance. How she hated herself for the conclusion she had drawn so hastily from the postscript of Margaret's letter, and how unreasonably bitter she felt against Margaret for writing it! And yet she could hardly wish that it had been left altogether unwritten. It had been worth while—it *was* worth while to suffer as she was suffering, to have had twenty-four hours of such supreme happiness first.

She thought she grasped fully the significance of his act, but she could not feel sure of the motives which had prompted it. She could conjecture many, but none satisfied her wholly. The most plausible seemed that he could not altogether pardon her the part she had played towards his lost Stella; and though the vivid recollection of what had passed at their last meeting in Oxford seemed to contradict such a supposition, she got over the contradiction by assuring herself that he had then been carried away by a flood of chivalrous compassion which had temporarily overpowered every other feeling. In calmer moments he had judged her differently; and perhaps her culpable weakness on that miserable day had helped him to a sterner judgment concerning her. She could not, perhaps would not, face the possibility that the love he had so long felt for her might simply have died a natural death, swallowed up by the tide of his advancing ambition, or swept out of existence by the current of a newer fancy.

However this might be, her visions were all at an end—her vague confidence in the future, her eager looking forward to the end of her journey, her exquisite shadowy anticipation of undefined happiness awaiting her in England, all were alike gone. Helen Bretherton grew uneasy at last at the change in her darling—at Muriel's sudden lapse into silence and indifference, and at the total cessation of her newly revived interest in men and things. Her uneasiness increased when she found that Frederic Earle's visit, on which she had counted so much, availed nothing to lighten the weariness and depression from which Muriel suffered, and that Muriel seemed only too glad to find excuses for sending him away with Marjory St. John on every possible occasion, and remaining alone with her own thoughts, which, if anything might be gathered from her face, could not be very happy ones. Helen made one attempt to gain Muriel's confidence on the subject of her secret trouble, but was so firmly, albeit gently, repulsed that she dared not try to repeat the experiment.

Once or twice an uncomfortable misgiving crossed Miss Bretherton's mind as to whether her diplomacy had been quite successful in promoting Muriel's happiness, but she quickly put the misgiving aside. She was so perfectly persuaded that it could not be for Muriel's advantage to have anything to do with Wentworth, and so entirely convinced that she must be in love with young Earle, that she declined to reproach herself for her crooked dealings, and argued that the pale face and sad, listless manner which grieved her could only be induced by the distress Muriel must feel at witnessing the faithless Earle's growing devotion to the obnoxious Miss St. John, with whom he was certainly indulging in a very promising flirtation. " My poor darling is so proud that she chooses to encourage it," said Helen indignantly to herself, " but it is breaking her heart all the same."

They lingered long on their homeward road, for Muriel seemed to have lost all desire to reach England quickly, and Helen had never been eager to get back early in the summer. So it came to

pass that July had begun before they reached
London and parted company, Miss Bretherton
returning to her modest mansion at Oxford, and
Muriel going down to her old home at Alderton,
where only her father was left to welcome her
now. As Helen sat looking out at the rich
green meadows between Reading and Taplow,
she found herself wishing more decidedly than
she had ever done before that she had not expressed herself quite so definitely at Cadenabbia
on the subject of Muriel's contemplated marriage.
Then her engagement had seemed to Helen a
certainty, to be proved in a few days' time; and
now, whatever else was uncertain about Muriel.
it was quite certain that she was not engaged to
Mr. Earle, and might never be engaged to him,
since he had apparently transferred his fickle
affections to Miss St. John. And here a new
idea suddenly darted into Helen's brain. Was
it Marjory who had been the attraction all along?
The girl had been a daily visitor at the Villa
Chiara during the previous winter: was it her
presence which had been the real magnet regu-
lating the young *attaché's* comings and goings?
Helen turned faint with dismay as this solution
of at least part of the mystery burst upon her
mind. Had Muriel been deceived like herself,

or had she seen clearly all the time at what shrine Mr. Earle was really paying his devotions?

Well, it was too late to go back now. Helen was far too great a coward to provoke Muriel's wrath by a confession of what she had done, for she guessed instinctively that the moment of her confession would be the last of Muriel's confidence in her; and she could not endure the thought of losing her cousin's confidence. Still less had she any intention of humbling herself before Wentworth, and thus leading to the very catastrophe she had plotted and prevaricated to avert. Yet she was desperately uncomfortable, and could only comfort herself by reflecting that the harm done was not, after all, very great. She had at least succeeded in delivering Muriel from the unscrupulous wiles of a man she thoroughly detested, but whom—much as she disliked him —she believed she could trust to hold his tongue on the subject of the pseudo-engagement. Helen felt instinctively that she might trust to Wentworth's honour to keep the secret she had imparted to him in confidence; and she had never positively stated to him that Mr. Earle was the man to whom Muriel was "about to be married." If he had chosen, from other remarks of hers, to infer as much, that was his affair; he could not proclaim his inferences as a fact. So Helen argued with herself, and was mightily comforted. She would indeed have felt quite happy, but for a certain sense of resentment against fate for having placed her in the position of a forger of unlikely falsehoods, when she had only meant honestly to tell the truth—by anticipation. Just so, poor Helen. It was the anticipation which created all the disorder.

Muriel, as has been said, had gone straight to Alderton, declining all the hospitable invitations of Lady Ellesthorpe and Margaret Irvine to halt in town on her way. She had a nervous horror now of accidentally crossing Wentworth's path, and so seeming to force upon him the meeting he had taken such pains to avoid. Even her rapid transit across London from station to station was full of terrible possibilities to her, and it was not until she found herself safe within the familiar walls of the Manor House that she felt secure from the chance encounter which, a few weeks earlier, she had reckoned upon as one of the blissful probabilities of her return, and the very idea of which had suddenly become unendurable.

It so happened, however, that she had to go to London after all. There were certain formalities to be gone through in connection with the little

property left her by her godmother, which absolutely required her presence in town for a time.
Thither, therefore, she went at the beginning of
August, gladly consenting to make Lady Ellesthorpe's house her home during her brief stay, on
the sole condition that her hostess would not
insist on her going anywhere or seeing any one.
And to this condition Lady Ellesthorpe agreed
readily. "Indeed, I should have hard work to
find means of breaking the compact," she wrote
in reply, "for there is nobody left in London
now but a few wretched M.P.'s, whose wives and
families, less devoted than myself, have already
fled, and left them to their dreary fate."

When Muriel had been in town a few days,
however, there was a sudden burst of excitement—"got up," Lord Ellesthorpe told her,
"expressly for her benefit, it seemed to him."
A rather irresponsible but prominent member
of the Opposition—"a leader of the free-lances,"
Lord Ellesthorpe called him—gave notice to
move a vote of censure on the Government
in re some of their recent acts in Wales, and
Ministerial whips went forth to the north, south,
east, and west, to summon absent members for
this unexpected debate and division of importance. "You had better go with my wife to-

morrow night and hear it," Lord Ellesthorpe said to Muriel. "It will probably be worth hearing. Lynwood" (the "free-lance") "is always racy, and there will be one or two other good speakers on his side, and Orme and Carew on ours—to say nothing of Wentworth himself, who is always at his best when attacked."

Muriel grew pale with agitation. The temptation was undoubtedly very great; and surely she might, with a little precaution, get to the Ladies' Gallery without any risk of encountering Wentworth by the way. But she would not allow herself to give an answer on the spur of the moment. She only thanked Lord Ellesthorpe evasively, and said she would talk to Lady Ellesthorpe about it.

That afternoon she had to drive to Lincoln's Inn to see her lawyer, and it must be supposed that during her drive she made up her mind on the subject of Lord Ellesthorpe's proposition, for as soon as she returned, she went straight to his wife's room and told her of it. Would Lady Ellesthorpe go? She herself would like to go very much.

Lady Ellesthorpe was perfectly willing to go, and manifested some surprise at Muriel's thanking her for falling in with the plan. "I am on fire to go myself, my dear," she said. "I have been gradually getting bored to death for lack of a little excitement lately; and I shall thoroughly enjoy hearing our opponents get the worst of it, as on this question they certainly will. Mr. Lynwood will first amuse us with his reckless impertinences, and then we shall have the pleasure of witnessing the process of his grinding to powder at the hands of Mr. Wentworth, who will sit down, when the operation is over, with his usual magnificent air of scorn. I like that air; I should think it must be more galling to the honourable gentleman who has just been pulverized than Wentworth's most cutting sarcasms—there is a lofty fatigue about it which seems to say, 'After all, that pigmy was not worth the trouble of arguing with.' I should have been very angry with you, Muriel, if you had not cared to go; Ellesthorpe told me at luncheon that he thought you were inclined to be perverse on the subject, so I am glad you have seen fit to come to a better frame of mind."

Muriel smiled faintly and flushed hotly. The decision she had come to was the result of a very simple circumstance: she had seen Wentworth that afternoon. He had swept rapidly past her in his brougham on his way to Westminster, and although he had not recognized her—he was at the moment looking over some papers he had just extracted from his despatch-box—this passing glimpse of him had awakened all the old irresistible craving for the sight of his face and the sound of his voice. "He will never know "— that was how she tried to salve her pride—"and there is nothing out of the way in my going; it is quite natural that I should feel an interest in the debate. I dare say I might have gone in any case." Poor Muriel! all her troubles had left her just as much of a woman as ever.

Afterwards she said that the scene of that evening always seemed to her more like a dream than anything else. The eager watching as the House gradually filled, when, from having at first been able to mark the entrance of each several member, she was perforce obliged, as the crowd grew greater, to confine her attention to the neighbourhood of the Treasury Bench itself; the sudden instinctive consciousness that *he* was among that serried group of men close by the Speaker's chair, and the ensuing vehement anxiety, amounting almost to agony, for his companions to move that she might be able to confirm herself in her belief that he was there; the sudden dispersion and movement of the group in different directions, its members falling into new groups and combinations like the pieces of glass in a shaken kaleidoscope, and when these had consolidated themselves once more, the sight of Wentworth's tall figure standing in the gangway holding a brief consultation with one of his colleagues—all these recollections partook more or less of a phantasmagoric nature. She could not remember what followed much more clearly. She knew that Mr. Lynwood spoke for a long time, his speech being, as it seemed to her, a mixture of violent invective and more or less inappropriate buffoonery—which latter ingredient, at any rate, had the desired effect of putting the House in good humour—and that throughout the speech Wentworth sat perfectly quiet and unmoved, only glancing now and then at his notes, and sometimes gazing at the ceiling of the House as if he found the flood of virulent abuse simply wearisome. She was vaguely aware that Mr. Lynwood was followed by some one else on his own side of the House, who spoke in the same strain, but more soberly—as well he might, being a very "responsible" leader indeed, not of the free-lances, but of the Opposition itself; that Mr. Orme replied; and that the next speaker was a "National" whose harangue was frequently interrupted by disputes with the chair concerning points of order. This speaker's utterances roused her partially from her semi-entranced condition. Among other pleasantries of like nature, he alluded to a little scene which had taken place at question time, and to an expression of regret then uttered by Wentworth that certain instructions of his touching the suppression of disorderly political meetings should have been so worded as to be capable of misconstruction, by observing that "though Welshmen fully appreciated the touching sensitiveness of the right honourable gentleman's conscience, and had never failed to admire the frankness with which he seemed always ready to join his ancient namesake of Tarsus in proclaiming himself the chief of sinners both in his public and private career, yet they were beginning to grow a little weary of these fulsome expressions of a penitence which led to no amendment of life." Then Muriel glanced at Wentworth, and saw that he never stirred or looked up; she heard the Nationals cheering boisterously, amidst cries of "Order!" and counter-cheers from the Ministerial benches; Lady Ellesthorpe whispered in her ear, "This happens so often that I don't suppose he cares;" and in a moment more a significant hush fell upon the excited assembly. Wentworth was at the table, and had actually commenced his reply.

Men who were in the habit of hearing Wentworth speak told Muriel afterwards that the speech in answer to Lynwood was the finest he ever made. She herself could have given but a poor account of its subject matter, so thrilled, so shaken, so transported out of herself was she by the mere sound of that voice which had won her girlish heart with its first accents, and which she now heard in all its full power and beauty and matchless variety as she had never heard it before. Hitherto she had known only a few notes of the instrument; now she seemed to hear all its strings vibrating one after the other. The tones in which Wentworth delivered his opening statement were calm and clear and silvery; but they waxed deeper, gathering to themselves an inflection of piercing scorn, as he made his overwhelming refutation of the accusations brought against the policy of the Government he represented, and rising gradually to an indignant climax, broke out into full volume in the majestic passion of his peroration, when he called upon the House to reject the vote of censure sought to be passed upon himself and his colleagues for crimes of which they had never been guilty. Whether he sat down again with the "magnificent air" of which Lady Ellesthorpe had spoken, Muriel could not say: her eyes were too dim to see him at all just then. She only knew that there was a great outburst of frantic applause, the House being fairly roused to one of its rare fits of excitement; that soon afterwards she was told that the debate had been adjourned, and that it was time to go home; that she stumbled to her feet somehow, and went down the narrow staircase, walking as if in her sleep; and did not come entirely to herself till she had driven away with Lady Ellesthorpe in the cool night air, and heard her companion lament the mischance that had prevented her being able to congratulate Wentworth on his performance. "Did you not see?" she asked Muriel. " He drove away just as we came out. Very inconsiderate of him; people ought to stay to be congratulated when they have made such speeches as that! I had all manner of pretty things ready to say to him, which will spoil utterly by keeping." Muriel had not seen Mr. Wentworth, she said. She could only hope earnestly in secret that he had not seen her.

Well, she had heard him, and she had learnt to her cost that she must never do so any more, if she could possibly help it. If life—such a life of duty and patience as she desired to live—were to be possible to her, there must be no more draughts of such a sweet and deadly elixir as she had drunk that night, no more surreptitious snatching of delights which awoke in her such a tumult of rebellious feeling as she could not have believed it within the bounds of possibility she should ever again experience. The daring experiment she had made must never, never be repeated, if she was to have any hope at all of attaining eventually to that peace of mind which was her sole ambition now. She must run no unnecessary risk of being forced to see or hear Wentworth again.

For this reason she excused herself from visiting Margaret at Margaret's own house, though she welcomed her friend gladly at Lady Ellesthorpe's. But for all Muriel's glad welcome and clinging warmth of affection, Margaret knew that the barrier which had risen up between them two years earlier was not yet broken down. Muriel puzzled her almost as much as Paul— Paul, who had come back from the journey which Margaret had fondly hoped was to put him right with himself and the world a sadder and older and more careworn man than he set out. It was all very sad and very strange; but after Margaret had seen Muriel, the sadness and the strangeness of it seemed greater and more inexplicable to her than ever.

CHAPTER XVI.

"YOURS, AND THE WORLD'S, AND GOD'S."

" Yet in these ears, till hearing dies,
    One set slow bell will seem to toll
    The passing of the sweetest soul
    That ever look'd with human eyes."

TENNYSON.

IT is April on the Western Riviera: and can
anything, I ask you, be more serenely beautiful,
more tranquilly satisfying to the senses, than
such an April day as this? The sky overhead
is dazzlingly blue; the sea below, its sparkling
expanse broken here and there by jets and
crestlets of foam literally white as milk, is blue
also, ranging in hue from the deepest indigo
near the narrow beach, where the sturdy Bordighera fishermen are sleepily mending their nets
or dozing frankly in the glorious laughing sunshine, through numberless gradations and shades
and semitones of colour to palest turquoise on

the far horizon. On the hills the olives, stirred by the soft southern breeze, are turning their silvery under-leaves to the sun, losing all their sadness of aspect for the moment, and the grim stone-pines scattered among them are bursting into fresh shoots of tender green, and the famous palms of Bordighera, released from the long winter captivity which was to blanch them for the Easter festival at Rome, are gladly flinging out their great fans to the light and air. Here and there the wild peach trees show themselves, laden with brilliant bloom, while in some sheltered spots by the tiny rivers which run through every valley—baby rivers whose only work in life is to laugh and dance perpetually among fallen boulders and over smooth white stones till they tumble heedlessly into the sea, adding yet one more shade to its endless kaleido-scope of colour—a sweet strong fragrance will guide you to the orange blossom which is just venturing to unfold itself. Among the olive terraces themselves you may walk almost on a carpet of flowers. The "faint frail wood violet's" day is nearly done, albeit her showier relative of Parma still flourishes in the violet gardens of Taggia fifteen miles away, but as far as eye can see are myriads of the delicate white narcissus of the poets; while brilliant anemones, red and blue, double and single, are blooming in the shadier spots where the fierce sun has not yet been able to reach and wither their fragile lives, and you can gather handfuls of tall scarlet tulips, and of their more delicate lady sisters, at your will. Down beside those stepping-stones over the bed of the torrent, there is a nodding company of starry pale yellow jonquils, and the rock behind them is clothed with a curtain of maidenhair kept continually fresh by the leaping spray. The cicalas have begun to chirp in the sun, and even high up among the terraces you can hear the faint wash of the sea below, mingled with a snatch of Italian folk-song from some boatman less sleepy or more musically inclined than his fellows. Old Bordighera slumbers on the hill, very grey and silent to contemplate from a distance, though within the narrow precipitous streets—veritable staircases many of them, up and down which men and women, mules and donkeys, walk heavily laden with equal unconcern—where the tall houses are strung together by arches leaving visible only a mere strip of sky, and perpetual shade reigns dark and cold, there is bustling, chattering life enough. New Bordighera is really silent, for there is little business doing to-day in the few shops which line the one "long unlovely street" of the town, and from the hotels and villas young men and maidens, invalids and children, have alike gone forth into the sunshine: either to gather anemones at Camporosso, or to sketch at Dolce Acqua, or to climb the steep ascent to queer, picturesque little Colla, where they will grope for a while in the strange picture-gallery which is dark even at midday, and look down on the white houses and red roofs of San Remo, lying between her two headlands on the other side of the hill, and finally wander home again through the lemon gardens of Ospedaletti when evening comes round. Some who do not care to extend their wanderings so far have contented themselves with the olive terraces nearer at hand. And, indeed, what can the eye of man desire better to dwell upon than the outlook from that nook among the olives towards the west, where we see Ventimiglia frowning on the hill-side, girt with her modest forts, and Mentone smiles shyly at us, nestling in her sheltered bay, and we can look past saucy little Monaco jutting out into the sparkling sea to the dim blue line of the Estérels beyond?

A party of people with whom we are more or

less concerned had chosen this last fashion of spending their Easter Tuesday, in the April of the year following that which had witnessed the failure of the last desperate attempt to upset the Coalition Government on the Welsh question. Lady Beatrice Orme, whose gallant exertions in keeping up her political *salon* had told rather seriously on her health of late, had been spending the winter at Bordighera, and now that the Easter holidays had released even Cabinet Ministers for a while from their labours, her husband had joined her there, bringing with him a whole contingent of friends to fill the pretty little Villa Vittoria, and cheer his wife's spirits after her lonely winter. They were a cheery company; young mostly, and all fairly light-hearted. The element of seriousness was only supplied by Paul Wentworth, who, travelling along the coast, had halted to see his friend and colleague, and had been hospitably persuaded to linger on. Even he, however, seemed to have caught the prevailing infection of gaiety from the season and the day; and while the *al fresco* luncheon was being discussed, he threw himself heartily into the spirit of the feast, and was once again, as in vanished days he had used invariably to be, the life and soul of the party.

They talked, as people will on these occasions, in a light, discursive fashion, touching now on this subject, now on that. At length the conversation drifted round to the want of society at Bordighera, and some one asked Lady Beatrice if she had not found the winter intolerably dull.

"Not at all," she protested. "I wanted a genuine rest, you know; it was what I came here to get. And I had the children, who have been in Paradise for four months. Of course it was lucky that I felt no craving for gaiety, for that was certainly not procurable. I had a few friends at San Remo, but very few; most people one knows go to Cannes, you see."

"Any one I know at San Remo now?" inquired Mr. Orme, lighting a fresh cigar.

"Yes, the Seymours are there, and the Earles —no, I believe the Earles have gone on to Milan by this time—and the Cochranes are expected to arrive there this week. And then there is Mrs. Arlingham, who has been at the Villa Chiara all the winter."

"I should like to see Cochrane—you might write and ask him and Lady Mary to come over and dine and sleep one day, Bee. We have room, I suppose?"

"We could manage to squeeze them in, if you

really want them," answered Lady Beatrice in a wifelike manner.

"And Jack Arlingham's widow is there, you say? Poor little soul! she must have a dull life of it now. She is not too well provided for, is she?"

"Rather better than I feared would be the case. She came into some money unexpectedly about the time of her husband's death—from an aunt, wasn't it, Mrs. Bernard?"

"Yes, an aunt of her father's, who had been her godmother, I believe," responded that young matron, who, with her husband, was among the Ormes' guests at Villa Vittoria.

"Does she live quite by herself? She is rather over young and pretty for that yet," remarked Mr. Orme. "Try one of these cigars, Wentworth; I can confidently recommend them."

"No," replied Lady Beatrice. "She and that odd Miss Bretherton—her elderly half-German cousin, you know—are keeping house on joint-stock principles. They have got an uncommonly pretty little villa at San Remo, off the most secluded part of the Berigo road. It is really a most charming little place—only, unfortunately, out of the way when one wants to go and call, and hasn't much time to spare."

"Mrs. Arlingham has nearer relations than Miss Bretherton living, surely?" said Wentworth interrogatively, joining for the first time in the conversation.

"Yes, but they are all out of reach in India, I think, except her father. I believe she spends her summers with him."

"I wonder if Muriel will ever marry again?" Mrs. Bernard said reflectively, after a minute. The assembly under the olives was now reduced to a quartet of members: herself, the Ormes, and Wentworth. The rest had wandered off in quest of fresh entertainment.

"Why not?" responded Mr. Orme, who was lying at full length on the grass, luxuriously enjoying his regalia. "She is young still, and, I suppose, pretty still—unless she has altered very much since I saw her last."

"She is more than pretty still, although I cannot say she is unaltered," Lady Beatrice said. "I hope she will marry some day."

"Well, I don't think sentimental consideration for Arlingham's memory need withhold her long," Orme observed. "I have no patience with a man who can marry a charming girl, and then behave to her as Arlingham did."

"I wish she would marry, too," Mrs. Bernard

chimed in. "But I rather doubt her doing it. For one thing, I think she has been almost too thoroughly saddened to have spirit to begin life afresh; and then she gives herself no chance of forgetting the past, leading such a secluded life as she leads now."

"She went about a little last autumn with Marjory St. John," Lady Beatrice remarked.

"That was purely for Marjory's sake. Muriel knew that Fred Earle—who is a distant cousin of the Arlinghams, I believe—was devotedly attached to the girl, and that Fred's people were against the match simply because her 'tocher' was not large enough. She happened to have some influence with old Mrs. Earle, and her patronage of Marjory was due chiefly to a desire to smooth the course of true love, which, by dint of unwearied efforts, she successfully did at last."

"Then the engagement is formally allowed?"

"Yes, and they are to be married in June. —Mr. Wentworth, will you kindly hand me my sunshade? The leaves are not wholly efficient as a screen, I find. Thanks. Won't you come into the shade yourself? You look as if you were finding the heat a little *too* delightful, and Lady Beatrice and I both positively enjoy the scent of a cigar."

"It is not too hot for me, thank you," Wentworth answered briefly.

"If Phœbus Apollo is going to treat us to
much more of this," quoth Mr. Orme from his
recumbent position, "I shall decline Apricalla
altogether. So if you wish your husband to
make one of your picnic-party, Bee, you had
better set it on foot before it grows any hotter."

"I am quite prepared," Lady Beatrice averred.
"Shall we say to-morrow?"

"You are really promptitude and willingness
to oblige itself," returned her husband, giving
her an affectionately admiring glance from under
the tilted brim of his hat. "In recognition of
which admirable qualities, I will not make even
a single counter-proposition. We *will* say to-
morrow—at least, if Mrs. Bernard says so too?"

Mrs. Bernard proved equally complaisant.
"And the Right Honourable Paul Wentworth—
what does he think on the subject? Will the
affairs of Taffy permit themselves to be neglected
for a whole day?"

"I think so," replied Wentworth, with a smile.
"I am trying to forget Taffy's existence for a
while, in so far as he will allow me to do so.
And on the whole he has shown himself pretty
considerate of late."

But when, at eight o'clock next morning, Lady Beatrice reviewed her party—a contingent of which was gaily but uncomfortably mounted on donkeys—before they started on their distant expedition, Wentworth was missing from the ranks. "Where's the cruel oppressor of the down-trodden Cymri?" she inquired merrily of her husband, as he issued from the villa clad in mountaineering garb, and carrying a formidable stick. "Is he inditing one of his barbarous despatches to his servile emissaries in Wales? If so, I hope he won't be long about it."

"I'm sorry to say he is not coming."

"Not coming? Shameless renegade!"

"He begged me to make his excuses to you, and hoped you would receive them in a Christian spirit. He has got several letters to answer—I can vouch for them, Bee, for I saw them myself—and this afternoon he wants particularly to go over to San Remo, to call on a friend there."

"Do you know who the friend is?" asked Lady Beatrice, whose curiosity was easily roused.

"No, I don't. Wentworth did not tell me," replied Mr. Orme, turning aside to tighten the strap of one of his gaiters. But a smile crossed his face as he spoke. Perhaps among the olives on the previous day he had observed more

through his half-shut eyelids than he chose to
communicate, even to his wife.

His scarcely formed suspicions were in the
main correct. When towards three o'clock Wentworth started off on foot along the beautiful
stretch of road which lies between Bordighera
and San Remo, his sole object in visiting the
latter place was to see Muriel Arlingham. Since
Mrs. Bernard's careless words the day before had
shown him how greatly he had been deceived—
wilfully, he began to think, for it had been
impossible to mistake Helen Bretherton's drift
when she spoke to him of young Earle at Cadenabbia, or to forbear seeing that her words on
that occasion had each been carefully weighed
before they were uttered—he had had but one
thought and desire, to see Muriel. He did not
go further than this at present. What had induced Miss Bretherton to weave a plot in order
to separate Muriel and himself, how Muriel would
now receive him, what he should say to her
when they met, what he hoped and intended to
come of the interview, or if he had any hopes
and intentions at all—upon none of these questions did he hold converse with himself. He
must see her—that was all. But how should he
find her ? Altered, saddened, too heart-broken

for hope—this was what they said of her. Was
it his apparent forgetfulness and faithlessness
which had saddened her ? Had the act of renunciation, wrought in a very anguish of self-
immolation wholly for her beloved sake, been
converted by a malignant fate into the deadliest
of wounds dealt her by his own hand ? Was his
crowning deed of reparation become, in fact, no
reparation at all, but, on the contrary, the infliction of a new and worse injury ? This was
indeed bitter, passing bitter! Well, he should
see her; and even if she turned from him in
anger, it would be something to have looked on
her face again.

He went swiftly along the broad beaten track,
breasting the long hill leading up from Ospedaletti without break or pause, and never stopping
once to heed the exquisite surroundings of his
way. The pleasant breeze of the day before had
swelled to something like a gale during the night,
and though the wind had now gone down and
the leaves of the olives hung pensively motionless, the sea had not yet subsided into calm. It
broke on the Capo Nero in sheets of foam, and
flung itself scornfully accross the slender *molo*
which at San Remo affords the sole shelter that
dangerous anchorage offers to passing vessels

from the fierce Mediterranean storms. It was no
longer blue, but a palish green in colour, with
shifting opalescent lights flickering all about its
surface, and here and there strange belts and
streaks of wonderful browns and reds where the
mountain torrents had coloured it with the soil
they brought down with them or the recent
storm had churned up the depths below. But
landward all was calm. Only at long intervals
came that gentle rustle among the olives which
of all inanimate sounds is most like a human
sigh; the white villas of San Remo had basked
so long in the sun that their red roofs seemed
positively incandescent with his rays, and even
on the lofty plateau above the Old Town, where
the church of the Madonna della Costa stands
white and glittering, there was not a breath of
air to stir the drooping branches of the trees.
The road was almost deserted, except for a few
peasant women trudging sturdily along, with
their great baskets full of olives balanced fear-
lessly on their well-poised heads, and an occasional
country cart laden with wood, dragged by a string
of mules in queer ornate harness, gaily decorated
with bells, squirrels' tails, and pheasants' feathers,
and directed by a countryman who cracked his
whip, and sang " Oje Caruli," and flung himself

into all manner of picturesque attitudes in keeping with the tenor of his song, solely for his own
amusement by the way. Carriages full of tourists
were few and far between. On such a day
people had evidently given the palm to up-
country excursions.

On the Berigo road itself—at least, on that
portion of it where Wentworth had been told he
should find Muriel's villa—was absolute solitude
and silence. The house was about half-way up
the slope of the hill, looking west, and a little
withdrawn from the road itself, to which it stood
at right angles. From the gate Wentworth
looked across a ravine far below the level of the
road, where a noisy unseen torrent could be
heard flowing and foaming, to a beautiful range
of heights, terraced with olives to their very
summits; and, lit up by the westering sun, La
Colla gleamed like a jewel set on the forehead
of the mountain beyond. Turning in, he found
himself in a garden where the roses were already
in full bloom, and the orange trees only waiting
to burst into blossom beside them; while over
the pillared colonnade in front of the low one-
storied white house, a graceful wistaria and a
Banksia covered with flowers were disputing the
precedence with one another in tangled profusion.

Just such a home as he would have chosen for
her; such a home as he would be glad to picture
her in, during all the years——

But an Italian maid had opened the door. Yes,
the Signora was at home—the Signora Arlingham?—*sì, sì, sì*. Would his Excellency give
himself the pain to walk in?

No, his Excellency would not do that just yet.
He wished first to know if the Signora was quite
disengaged. This determination he expressed in
fluent Italian to the handmaiden, who seemed
equally astounded at the determination and the
fluency, and finally prevailed upon her, not without difficulty, to carry his card to her mistress
leaving him still at the door.

In two minutes the girl came back. La
Signora was at liberty, and would be glad to
see his Excellency. Would he give himself the
pain to walk in *now?* She ushered him briskly
into the drawing-room, and there left him.

Wentworth looked hastily around. He was
in a small square room with two long French
windows, one opening on the colonnade with
its mantle of roses and wistaria, and the other
looking out over the ravine to the west. It was
just such a villa drawing-room as may be found
by hundreds nowadays all along the coast of

Ligurian Italy, speaking distinctly enough of modest means, but beautified by a taste which knows how to make use of small prettinesses— of a bit of graceful drapery, a fragment of Florentine brasswork, or even of a mere branch of spreading mimosa in a Vallauris jar valuable only for its perfection of shape. But to Wentworth the room was eloquent of Muriel. Her music was open on the piano; her books were piled on the table; a piece of unfinished work, with the needle hanging from it, lay beside a closed letter which bore her hand-writing. All this Wentworth saw in a flash of time, as it were, for he had hardly been a moment alone when the door re-opened and Muriel herself came in, a tall slim figure in a pale grey dress, with ruffles of soft lace at her throat and wrists.

Friends who have been long separated, and between whom any kind of barrier has arisen, rarely meet in actual life with much visible emotion. Wentworth and Muriel formed no exception to the general rule. They greeted each other calmly enough as far as outward seeming went, and Muriel said, " I am very glad to see you. Will you sit here?" much as she might have uttered those commonplace formulæ to any other morning visitor.

"I am staying for a few days with the Ormes at Bordighera," Wentworth said, " and as I heard you were residing here, I thought I might venture to call. I am fortunate in having found you at home."

"I am very glad I happened to be at home," Muriel answered. "It is just a chance that I did not go to Ceriana this morning; Miss Bretherton, my cousin, who lives with me—or I with her—has driven over there for a day's sketching."

She spoke very calmly, and her calmness gave Wentworth a mortal chill. Now that they had actually met, a gulf greater and more impassable than any which had separated them previously, seemed to have suddenly opened between them. How could he guess that Muriel had lived so long in the habitual repression of feeling that she felt incapable of allowing any emotion to show itself? How could he know that, even while she uttered the words which to him seemed so cold, she was crying out in her heart, "Thank God! thank God! I have not missed him;" that her eyes were noting wistfully how thin was the hand which had clasped hers for one blessed moment, and that she had hard work to keep down her tears when she saw how heavily dashed with grey were the thick waves on his temples?

"Are you not fond of excursions?" he asked, with a strange sinking of the heart.

"As a rule I enjoy them very much. But I know all this neighbourhood pretty intimately— and this morning I had a headache. That was my real reason for shirking the expedition."

"I hope it is a reason which does not often occur with you? I was thinking you looked well—on the whole," he added doubtfully; for, though his eyes could recognize no diminution of beauty in the face which for ten years he had deemed the fairest on earth, he could not but perceive that it had lost in roundness and colour.

"I am well—very well," Muriel answered, with a quick blush which for an instant revived all the memory of her earliest and most beautiful bloom. "And you yourself, Mr. Wentworth? I am sure your office is one which must tax any strength."

"Plenty of hard work, with a due admixture of occasional excitement," Wentworth answered, with a slight smile. "I don't think it has disagreed with me until this spring, when I certainly felt a little out of sorts, and good old Falconer was very anxious that I should try a run abroad. I believe he was right: I shall probably go home new-made after a fortnight of this Paradise, and 'set my ruthless heel on the Principality'—isn't that the last correct phrase? —with renewed vigour for the rest of the year."

"The summer before last must have been a terrible one for you," Muriel observed. She could not answer him in his own tone; the unchanged look of patient pain in his face was wringing her heart too deeply.

"It was trying. But at times I rather enjoyed it too. Those who have never tried it cannot imagine how exhilarating it becomes occasionally to feel that you walk about with your life in your hand; you find yourself setting quite a new and fictitious value on the continuance of your own existence after a little while." Went- worth spoke with a touch of his old recklessness.

"It was terrible, terrible!" Muriel repeated in a tremulous voice—the first faint sign of emotion Wentworth had been able to descry in her. "But all that is at an end now?"

"For the present, wholly at an end. Things are steadily quieting down, and I hope we shall not have to ask for any renewal of our extra- ordinary powers."

"That is something," Muriel said, with a sigh— was it a sigh of relief? "And is your holiday to be a long one? Are you going further on into Italy?"

"I may run over and refresh my recollections of Genoa, perhaps; I shall not have time for anything more, for I must start homewards on Saturday."

"Is your daughter Mabel with you?" Muriel inquired. "I should like very much to see her."

"No, she is not with me," he answered— Muriel fancied, a little sadly. "I should like to have brought her out, but she had one or two invitations she was very anxious to accept in England. Perhaps we may do a little travelling together in the summer instead; but I don't think very young girls care generally for travelling—do you? It is rather a taste which comes with maturer years. Mabel prefers those pleasures which lie near home at present."

"I don't know; I used to be very fond of it in my younger days," Muriel replied. "But I have done so much of it during the last few years, that now I am glad to rest."

"You have chosen a charming resting-place, at all events," Wentworth said. "This is almost an ideal villa, I think."

"It is rather small, but very sweet and home-like, and the garden is a great delight all through the winter. Did you see my heliotrope hedge to the right as you came in ? Look out of the window behind you, and admire it, please ! Miss Bretherton and I are very proud of that heliotrope hedge : it is considered quite the finest in San Remo !"

Wentworth got up and opened the window wider in order to get a better view of the famous hedge. It was in full bloom, and a little puff of wind carried a strong breath of the spicy fragrance into the room, and awoke in him the recollection of another day ten years ago, when Muriel had bent in girlish rapture over the flowers he had brought her—his first and only gift. " It is exquisitely pretty," he said, turning back, and meeting something in her eyes that set his heart beating madly. Had she remembered that day too ?

" Miss Bretherton deserves all the credit of its beauty," Muriel said, recovering herself instantly. " She is head gardener—she rules out of doors and I within, and so we go on in perfect harmony." She wondered why Wentworth should frown so unmistakably at this mention of her cousin.

" She is your constant companion, then ? " he responded in a voice which sounded rather harsh

"She is with me in the winter and spring. It is fortunate that she is at liberty to leave home at will, for I have no one else of whom I could make a *Hausgenossin*, as the Germans say."

"You had a sister who was not very strong, I think," Wentworth adventured. "Is she in India still?"

"Yes, she is still there, and likely to remain there. She is still extremely delicate; but in India she can help certain work, useful work, a little, while at home she would probably be quite an invalid. She is so anxious to be useful," said Muriel, with a quiver in her voice, "and all the doctors say her life *cannot* be a very long one. And my brother and sister-in-law are in India too. I have only my father in England—perhaps you do not know he is married again?—and even home is not quite what it once was. So if it were not for my kind cousin, I might be a little—lonely."

"But you have many friends?"

"Very many, I am happy to say; only the best friends cannot quite take the place of one's own people. Sometimes I have thought I would go out to India myself——" She stopped, colouring deeply, and quite unnecessarily, for how was Wentworth to guess that what had hitherto withheld her from carrying out her idea was her reluctance to put so many thousand miles between herself and the country whose air he breathed, where his name was for ever sounding in men's mouths, and where, perhaps, once or twice a year she might see him pass in the streets? " You have been in India, Mr. Wentworth, haven't you? Then perhaps you can tell me something about this place in the Punjaub, where my people are now? "

It so happened that he did know the place, and for the next quarter of an hour they talked only of that. Then he made a movement to go. A sick despair was at his heart. If Muriel had been cold or resentful, he would have tried to soften or appease her; but her gentle friend-liness held him back from any effort to approach her more nearly as nothing else on earth could have done.

She turned very pale as he rose. " Must you go? " she said falteringly. " It is a long walk from Bordighera; I am sure you must be tired. Miss Bretherton will not be long now. I thought you would perhaps have waited till she came back, and had some tea—— "

" Thank you, not to-day," Wentworth answered formally. "The Ormes have some people to dinner to-night, and I should not like to keep them waiting for me."

Muriel offered no further remonstrance. "I am so glad to have seen you," she said. It seemed impossible to get beyond that poor phrase.

"You are very kind to say so. I feared you might think it strange that I should have omitted to call upon you at Cadenabbia last year. Did you know that I was at Cadenabbia in May?"

"Yes. I—I heard so."

"And you did think it strange? Well, I had a very grave reason for not calling—I entreat you to believe me, Mrs. Arlingham, for this is a very serious matter to me—a very grave and sufficient reason. I came to Cadenabbia—to be perfectly frank—for the express purpose of seeing you. On my arrival I was informed of a fact—it now proves to be no fact at all, but a falsehood, and, I think, a malicious one—which convinced me that I had better have stayed away. Yesterday I learnt, for the first time, that I had been deceived, and that the story I speak of was untrue."

"What was it?" The words broke from her unawares, between two fluttering breaths.

"I suppose there is no reason why I should not tell you what it was. I was informed that you were going to be married shortly, and therefore I felt it to be a moment when I had better not intrude upon you. The visit of an outsider like myself could only have been a trouble to you. So I decided to—to stay away." He could not keep his voice quite steady to the last.

" How could you suppose—— " Muriel began, impulsively. But she checked herself quickly, if not altogether in time, and said more quietly, " That was the reason, then ? I—I had thought it was something quite different."

"Will you forgive me if I ask a question in my turn ? What did you suppose the reason to be ? "

Muriel's eyes fell to the ground at her feet. "That you had not forgiven me—that you found you could not forgive me the injury I did you years ago through your child. If you think I have forgiven myself—— "

"Hush!" Wentworth interrupted almost sternly. " Do you think I will let you blame yourself for the consequences of my sins—consequences which, in your divine pity for me, you tried vainly to avert ? Is this what you have been thinking

—that I stayed away because I *wished* to stay ?"

She answered not a word. Only as she stood before him with her head still bent, he saw her lips tremble.

"Muriel," he said gently, coming a little nearer, "you spoke just now of being lonely. Is it possible that all the while I have been keeping this bitter silence for your sake, you have wanted me ?"

Still no answer, unless that one swift look upward at his face served for one.

"Cannot you understand," Wentworth went on in the same gentle way, "that when they told me you had happiness at last before you, happiness with one who had youth, and a stainless name, and a bright blameless life to offer you, it was not for me to throw my shadow between you and him ? Even now that I know you free, I could not dare to speak as I am doing, unless in some sort, of your own will, you had stooped towards me: I am too unworthy. Do you want any further answer to the question why I did not come to you before ?"

She shook her head faintly, and there were tears on her eyelashes.

"A little love would have brought me to you

long ago," Wentworth added, losing command of himself a little, and taking her cold hands in his, " but a love as great as mine could only keep me away. I don't know what I am doing, talking of little and great—what are words to describe my love for you at all ? "

She was trembling so uncontrollably now that he put one arm about her—not caressingly, but as a support—and stood so, looking down at her with something like compassion mingling with the reverent, impassioned tenderness in his nobly transfigured face. .

" My child, my child," he said very gravely and calmly—and never did even Muriel herself guess the agony of conflict it cost him to preserve that calmness—" I want you to be very sure of yourself in this thing. You think you love me, I know ; but are you certain that it is me whom you really love ? Recollect what I am—a man fast growing old, with a miserable history behind me, and before me a future which must be always darkened by bitter repentance for the unalterable past. Is it such a one as this whom you love, dear, or is it some *eidolon* of your fancy whom you call by my name ? "

" You—only you."

" Knowing what you know," the grave, tender

voice went on, "can you still give yourself to me in faith and confidence ? Could you consent to be my wife without misgivings, Muriel ? "

" Without one."

He caught her close to his heart. "So you not only forgive all that has been," he said half audibly, bending over her, "but you can trust me utterly ? "

"Utterly, Paul, and in all things." Then he stooped still lower, and kissed her on the lips, as if to set seal on the troth she had given.

"Your faith is as wonderful as ever," he said at last, smiling rather sadly, and putting her a little from him in order to look into her sweet, radiant face. "It was always great, I remember, even in the darkest days. I had perforce to try and become worthy of it; I could not altogether disappoint such faith as yours—and little Stella's. But you have done very unwisely, child, when all is said. There is plenty of sunshine in the world; it is nothing but a noble madness that makes you choose to walk in the shadow with me."

"So long as it is with you," she replied hurriedly, "the rest matters very little, I think. Perhaps I may be able to lighten the shadow a little— and at least I can share it."

"Such love as yours carries its own brightness with it," Wentworth continued in a voice which he tried vainly to control. "And it might well be enough to make any man's life sunny. Yet —I dare not deceive you, my darling—there are some things that even your dear love cannot do. There is one grief at least that nothing can lessen. I would not forget Stella if I could—and I can never forget how I lost her."

For answer, Muriel put her arms about his neck, as simply and confidently as Stella herself might have done, and laid her head down again on his breast. "Dear," she said softly, "I do not ask you to forget. Though it breaks my heart to see you suffer so terribly, I can even believe that it may be right you should remember. All I hope is that God will let me comfort you a little."

THE END.

PRINTED BY WILLIAM CLOWES AND SONS, LIMITED,
LONDON AND BECCLES.   *G., C. & Co.*

www.ingramcontent.com/pod-product-compliance
Lightning Source LLC
Chambersburg PA
CBHW060554030726

47498CB00005B/1387

* 9 7 8 3 3 3 7 3 1 5 7 3 3 *